Inspector Foxglove

David Donahue

Copyright © 2018 David Donahue

All rights reserved.

ISBN: 9781983871030

1 A WATCH & CUFFLINKS	1
2 DOORS & WINDOWS	16
3 A RIDE IN THE NEIGHBOURHOOD	31
4 "SOMETHING OUGHT TO BE DONE"	43
5 THE APPEARANCE OF FOXGLOVE	57
6 THE COLOUR OF THINGS	70
7 THE VILLAINS AT TEA	84
8 REGARDING THE MOOR	95
9 IN ORDER TO PAY MR HAROLD A VISIT	109
10 MR RAMPERT IS MIRACULOUSLY CURED	127
11 THE DINNER PARTY	142
12 THE WOOING OF MISS PENELOPE PIMSLEUR BY MR NILES BLANKENSHIP	153
13 ON THE HEELS OF ORTON BLACK	167
14 THE FIRE WHICH CONSUMES	177
14A LETTERS BETWEEN CONSPIRATORS	191
14B LETTERS BETWEEN SISTERS	194
14C FATHER LEAMAS' SERMON	197

15 INSPECTOR FOXGLOVE, *CONSTABULE PRO TEMPORE*	**204**
16 PEN QUITS WESTWICH	**213**
17 THE DEVIL'S ELBOW	**224**
18 INTERVIEW WITH FATHER LEAMAS	**237**
19 THE STRANGE SUMMIT	**249**
20 THE WEATHER CHANGES	**266**
21 THE APOCAPLYPSE OF CALEB CHESWICK	**273**
22 ORTON BLACK AT LAST!	**278**
23 THE WEDDING DAY	**288**

1 A WATCH & CUFFLINKS

This is the story of the legendary battle of wits between the famous detective, Inspector Foxglove, and the infamous criminal, Orton Black; and how, in the end, the master criminal was brought to justice by the master detective.

It may be reassuring to the reader to know that in the end, things turn out alright. Even though we have ahead of us a story of thieves, murders, hidden treasures, tragic fires, broken hearts, troubled minds and fierce reprisals, we should say right off that things turn out just fine.

As a matter of course, we shall be introduced to a cast of characters- some we will love and others we might come to despise. Their hopes, their aspirations, their fears and loves will all become our own and as they rise, we shall rise and as they fall, we shall also fall. The path they tread into the valley of despair shall be our own path.

We will be discussing, in these pages, a number of grisly murders, an assortment of dastardly and underhanded robberies, the sad repercussions of ill-gotten gains, the nature of consuming and unrelenting fire, the shattered hopes of young people in love, and the effects of shocking mental instability but it is comforting to know it will all be just fine by the end.

The reader should prepare themselves to be a first-hand witness to the most egregious acts of human depravity; to consider in all the gory details the vilest and basest actions of men and women determined to wreak havoc on the lives of their fellow humans and to take it all with a grain of salt, knowing the end of the story will be as pleasant an end as one could hope for.

The sure promise of the destruction of all the goodness in one person's heart should not deter anyone from reading further. Instead, let the crushing weight of impending and inescapable doom act as a buoy of fortitude and a soothing balm to the reader, who knows with certitude this too shall pass.

Let us begin the story by reporting, in the spring of 1853, a string of robberies terrified the hamlet of Westwich and the surrounding neighborhood. Five separate households had been broken into and robbed over the course of several weeks and in each case, there was scant evidence to support the notion of robbery, except to say things of value were missing.

Let us explain.

The robberies- and there were robberies- all took place in local homes while the houses were occupied; either by the residents themselves or by the servant staff. There was, in no case, any explanation as to how someone could have gotten in unnoticed, let alone, moved through the house or indeed left the house with several items of value from rooms which were frequently occupied.

Certainly, each crime was troubling enough, but a few crimes of any size amounted to a crime wave in such a small country town. This was all something the small hamlet of Westwich and its surrounding neighbourhood was entirely unprepared for. Far to the north from London, and near the sea, Westwich was a small town whose nearest neighbor was another small town fifteen miles to the south and even that seemed too close for comfort.

This was a wide open part of the north country and visitors were seldom and few. Passersby would have to be quite lost to find their way to Westwich proper, though they may pass by on the outskirts on their way to somewhere else- but whom and to where? It would be anyone's guess.

Westwich was the sort of place where new faces would be recognised and new personal items wouldn't go unnoticed. Which is to say, relating to our current explanation of the facts of the crime wave, if one were to come into Westwich from the outside, people would notice; and, if one lived there already and suddenly owned new candlesticks identical to the ones Mrs B reported missing, well; people would notice that too.

Westwich was too remote for much of anything to really happen and, truly, no one in the neighbourhood could remember anything like one robbery ever happening in their lifetime or in their parent's lifetime. The old phrase, 'When it Rains, it Pours' was an idiom the people of Westwich had used time out of mind but now that they were witnessing it at work in their own backyard, so to speak, the well-worn phrase quickly fell out of local use by mutual and unspoken agreement.

For years and years, the town of Westwich and surrounding neighbourhood had been under the care and protection of a Constable by the name of Cheswick. Constable Cheswick had been a military man in his youth and due to a severe wound in battle, was discharged and sent home.

A military man with a lack of enemy can be a discouraging thing- without the Huns there would be no Wall of China, without the Normans there could hardly have been proper Saxons, without the Establishment there could never have been a Revolution- but having no enemy and no one to chase (while not helpful for an army) is also the mark of a very good Constable; and that is what Constable Cheswick was.

The people of Westwich had taken to saying Constable Cheswick 'kept the criminals away and the honest folk honest', and what they usually meant by it was anyone in Westwich who might have otherwise considered a life of crime, however limited in the small hamlet, was put off it by the presence of Constable Cheswick.

Who was this Constable Cheswick, you might ask? What manner of man was he to command the respect of citizen and would-be criminal alike? The plain answer is that it doesn't matter in the slightest because during the previous winter, prior to the spring in which the robberies began to take place, poor Constable Cheswick was taken with a cough and died quite suddenly. We have begun our story months after his death and the protection he might have provided would have ended our story before it began. Unfortunately, in this particular fact relating to the premature death of Mr Cheswick, there is a story to tell.

This was bad timing for crimes to occur; which is often the way of crimes and tragedy- there is generally no sense of propriety in the timing of such things. But, truth be told, it was probably not a coincidence, either. With the bulwark of Constable Cheswick no longer standing against the tides of crime in Westwich, perhaps it was an inevitable deluge which began next.

The death of the constable meant, in those days, that the son of the officer would take on the responsibilities of the office. Since the son- and the constable did have one- had been away at university studying botany, he was in no way considered prepared to take on the constabulary but duty and custom had prevailed over what might otherwise have been a successful and immediate transition to a qualified candidate for the open position of constable.

Instead, when the son returned to settle the estate of his late father, he stayed on and took up the office of constable, under the condition that a suitable and willing replacement should be found and the office transferred as soon and expediently as possible so that he might return to his studies with as little interruption as possible. Unfortunately, a position filled badly is still a position filled and the urgency which might otherwise contribute to a speedy transition faded without much discussion.

Mr Caleb Cheswick (that was the son's name) made it clear by word and deed he could not have been more disinterested in constabulary or law and as winter had passed and spring began announcing itself, he could often be found in the neighborhood around the hamlet and seen out on the edges of the moor (let the reader be warned the moor is where the Vagabonds are) with a walking stick in one hand and a botany book in the other, stopping on regular intervals to acknowledge and inspect the local flora, fauna and other niceties which make up a country spring, as seen through the eyes of a studious botanist.

It should be quickly noted here, however, that Mr Cheswick did comport himself admirably- if not quite ably- in his role as *constabule tempore* and when such duty did call him to action (if the normal activities of a country constable could properly be called action), he did it with a serious and dedicated air presumably borrowed from his botany studies- still holding his walking stick in the one hand but in the other, he would carry a volume entitled "*Manual of Dutief And Functionf Of A Conftable: a Handbook*", (further notated as the Third Edition by the venerable Messrs Green and Finchley). This manual he studiously followed to the letter in all constabulary-related matters. But it is a fact, and certainly no discredit to him, that when the burglaries of that spring in 1803 began he was, by all accounts, certainly in over his head, out of his depth and woefully undprepared. Thankfully for us, he also does not come into the story much and we do not need to give him any more description than this since he will soon be replaced by proper policing authorities and on his way back to university to study botany.

The story properly begins on the night Mr Pimsleur and his family arrived home late one night to find several items missing from Mr Pimsleurs own study room. The family, as a whole, had gone to Mrs B's for a dinner party- quite in fashion at the time- and had been gone from late afternoon till late evening doing the usual party things of talking and dancing and eating. Must a party be explained to the seasoned modern reader? Let us hope not. Only the servant staff was at home in the timeframe in which the crime must have been committed and they self-reported ignorance of the break-in (since there must have been one) to Mr Pimsleur.

So, the Pimsleurs had arrived home from a party to find their home broken into and robbed. Mr Pimsleur had no notion, intention or even a vague thought of accusing any of his own servants of stealing from him, much to his (and their) credit. The notion of dedicating one's life to serving another but then turning and stealing from that same individual was unthinkable, unspeakable and altogether incomprehensible. If anyone had suggested it, Mr Pimsleur would have waved it off and said, "Impossible."

No servant had entered Mr Pimsleur's rooms during the course of the evening in question, so there was no one to notice the items missing until Mr Pimsleur himself entered his rooms, exhausted from the party and vowing never to go to another party again as long as he lived- the only vow in his life he was known to break. After discovering the items were missing, he called his man to the fact and inquired whether the items were, perhaps, being serviced or simply misplaced?

A thorough investigation of these two possibilities commenced and within ten minutes it was determined there were no answers to be had down that line of inquiry and there may well have been criminal factors. (A factor which would have unthinkable in the past, but now there were several crimes in the past weeks). A servant was dispatched at once to town to fetch the constable and within three hours (it was now very late or very early in the morning) that temporary officer of the law was standing in the midst of the crime scene.

"Mr Pimsleur, when did you notice the items were missing?" said young Constable Caleb Cheswick.

"When we arrived home." said Mr Pimsleur.

"And where do you arrive home from?" said Constable Cheswick.

"From Mrs Bs" said Mr Pimsleur. "She was having a party."

"And what were you doing there?" said Constable Cheswick.

"My family and I were attending the fete-were you not invited?" said Mr Pimsleur.

"Oh, I was invited Mr Pimsleur, but the duty upon me did not permit my attendance. How was the fete?" said Constable Cheswick.

"It was, well, I suppose it was fine. I'm shaken by this robbery, truth be told. Such parties are not intended for old married men anyway." said Mr Pimsleur.

"Now, the robbery. Now, you say your family was with you at Mrs Bs?" said Constable Cheswick.

"Yes." said Mr Pimsleur.

"Can anyone verify your presence there?" said Constable Cheswick.

2 DOORS & WINDOWS

The Pimsleur Estate was the jewel of the neighbourhood. Its smooth lawns and manicured shrubbery were products of skill, patience, pride and, perhaps most importantly, a dedication to Mr and Mrs Pimsleur unrivalled by the staff of any other estate and reflecting in every detail the sensibilities of Mrs Laura Pimsleur. The gate (a very famous gate by the way), was wrought and carved in the manner of the classic style so popular at the time, but the gate doors themselves were, of course, always open. Elegant trees lined the long white gravel drive to the house and beyond, the tended gardens.

However, this description is all merely material detail which the reader can dream up or imagine on their own. What should be said is the Pimsleur estate was both the admiration and the envy of the neighbourhood. The smooth lawns which graced its surfaces was contoured in a way, so some said, as to provoke the fury of anyone who tried to emulate it- so precise and so lush. The manicured shrubbery was not to be so basely insulted as to be referred to as mere shrubbery; each botanical nomenclature was chosen to elicit a gasp of awe from even the most knowledgeable and well-travelled expert, not to mention the neighbors. The curated gardens, a half-dozen of them, did not merely draw on themes from Windsor, Noordeinde, Milan, Al-Hambra, Petrovsky Palace and others- no, each garden transported one to those very places.

In all, the Pimsleur Estate was the established goal of every other aspiring estate and homeowner in Westwich and surrounding neighborhood. Each estate on the moor looked to the Pimsleur as the standard of elegance and sophistication. Even Evelyn Winslow- who with her husband and eight children rented three cramped rooms and a shared bath on Clover St in Westwich referred to their window-box garden as 'Little Pimsleur'. Only the Blankenships did not admire the Pimsleurs- not out of a lack of envy, but out of a difficulty understanding how a family could be both admired and well-liked; to a family like the Blankenships, the possibility was quite unfathomable.

Early the next morning after the crime at the Pimsleur Estate, and resultant initial inquiry by the young constable, Mr Pimsleur and his wife were seated for breakfast and still waiting for their daughters to come down and join them when one of the housekeepers appeared to inform them that Constable Cheswick was in the front entry room, seeking Mr Pimsleur. Surprised to receive anyone so early, he rose and found the constable with only a small book in his hand, having left his walking stick on the front porch. Looking him over, Mr Pimsleur wondered whether the young man had slept at all in the few hours since he had seen him last.

"Good morning, constable. What can I do for you?" Mr Pimsleur said.

"Good morning, Mr Pimsleur. I beg your pardon- I hate to bother you this early in the morning- but I have been reading about my duties and I see that it is very necessary for me to look over the exterior of the house and especially the immediate area around the windows of the study. It may be the crook- rather, the suspect- had perhaps gained entry to the house through the window of the study, rather than the front door." the young constable said.

Mr Pimsleur had listened politely. He had determined, whatever his reservations about the constable's competency, to encourage the young man until proper help could arrive from the district authorities.

"Isn't it also possible, constable, that the suspect may have used any of the exterior doors or any of the other windows which are at ground level and accessible to an industrious criminal? That is to say, I hope you inspect all the windows and doors?" Mr Pimsleur said.

Constable Cheswick took this in with an attentive tilt of his head and then opened his book on constabulary duties. He turned a page or two and frowned. He looked up at Mr Pimsleur. Then the young man took a pencil from somewhere in his coat and made a careful note in the margin of his book. He closed it finally and said, "Yes, Mr Pimsleur. I shall check all the windows and doors on the ground level. With your permission?" Constable Cheswick said.

"You have full access, constable. Thank you for your service. Did you say last night you would be asking for help from the district?" Mr Pimsleur said.

"Oh, yes, sir. The pound value limitations on local cases means that I must contact the district and involve them. It appears that all these robberies are connected and in total, the value of the stolen items exceeds my responsibility." Constable Cheswick said.

"Yes- I think you mentioned that last night." Mr Pimsleur said.

"Quite as much, sir. Quite as much." Constable Cheswick said.

From where the two stood talking, one had a full view of the staircase which led to the second and third floors of the house. As they talked, a noise familiar to Mr Pimsleur (and thus, unnoticed) was heard by the young constable. He looked up the staircase at the sound of a door opening and a few short steps later, Penelope Pimsleur came into view at the top of the stairway. Catching sight of her, Mr Caleb Cheswick began making a thousand minute adjustments to his collar, making it look decidedly worse and all the while the corners of his constabulary book kept pressing into his face but with his attention so diverted, he could not source out the discomfort and continued the operation on his collar. Mr Pimsleur did not betray a single thought during this and did not think to tell the young man he was poking his own face with the book, assuming it was obvious.

A riddle and question arose in the mind of the young man: Who is this young lady, her white hand a guide, her fingers gently testing the waxen bannister? Who is she who wears her brown hair just so with care and carelessness in duet? Whose face, whose eyes? Whose slim shoulders and slender arms covered in muslin, shawled against the chill of a spring morning? Whose form descends, in each fluid movement, from on high to grace the mortal below? Whose steps, light and direct, point the way? Who is this young woman? Who is this who Caleb Cheswick once scoffed at as a child, and who now captures him at a glance? Who is this young woman who must never have before lived? Who is this? This is Penelope Pimsleur, and she was a riddle well worth solving.

You must understand; I love her more than anything or anyone. I do not mean merely that I love her more than I myself have personally loved before. No! I mean she is loved, I believe, more than anyone or anything in the entire history of our old world. I am fortunate to be the conduit for this blessed love- I cannot say it has its origin in me. I am too rough for that. I am not the deep aquifer; I am merely the well from which she draws. I am not the storm; I am merely the raindrop in her hand. Such is the woman I married. Or, so wrote her husband (who we may have chance to meet in these pages), years later on, after they married, to a friend in an attempt to express how he felt about her. In the meantime, Penelope Pimsleur was pleasantly unaware of such tributes in her future and was merely wondering, at that very moment, whether the breakfast scones might have any berries in them, it being so early in the year?

When Penelope had reached the bottom of the stair she did not approach the two men but turned abruptly into the kitchen, intent on scones. Indeed, with that one abrupt and unexpected movement, Cheswick wondered what exactly had changed- he only knew for certain something had changed.

It would be difficult to ascertain whether the windows needed so much inspecting for nearly all the rest of that morning or if he merely hoped to catch another glimpse of her but Constable Cheswick indeed took all morning inspecting the grounds, the doors and most especially the windows. In all, Constable Cheswick identified five external doors for entry and exit (the front, the rear, the kitchen and two ancillary which were not in common use and did not appear to have been used in the previous evening's crime), one cellar door which provided access from the interior to the exterior, but was locked from the inside and could not have been opened from the outside, and a total of eighteen windows which could conceivably be opened professionally in the event of criminal intent.

The ground beneath and round about each of the windows was checked for boot prints, or footprints or any prints which might suggest someone other than a member of the household had been nearby recently. But the dirt was cleanly raked the week before and only a cat had left prints under a few of the windows. The bushes, the shrubs and the flowers beds nearest the house suggested the same lack of human activities. In all, there was really no evidence beneath his boots for the constable to find.

There were two large oak trees nearest the house which might have served the criminal needs of an enterprising chimpanzee, Cheswick mused, but criminal chimpanzees were not to be considered seriously. It did occur to him, however, that all the items stolen from each of the homes were small enough a chimp might have easily carried them out. All in all, the windows at the ground level provided the most obvious entry for the thief.

Heavy is the head and weary the shoulders who bears the burden of duty and responsibility without actually understanding it. Constable Cheswick carried out the fullness of his duty in every respect. Those eighteen windows received the utmost attention. They were marvelously glazed and meticulously framed, it was certain, but even the glazier and framer did not spend so much time at one window as Cheswick did- but then, neither the glazier nor the framer had Miss Penelope Pimsleur in view from the other side.

Mid-morning overheard Mr Pimsleur speaking to his wife, "Well, Mr. Cheswick has been away at university long enough for Penelope to grow up- he didn't seem to recognize her at all. Otherwise, he is especially thorough, overmuch-so perhaps. He seems to be taking a lot of notes in his little book."

This may, in other stories, point to a budding affection and a promise of a future flowering romance between two young people, but since help from the district will soon arrive, and the young man will be headed back to university soon enough, we do not need to give much more thought to the tall young man who was so taken with Penelope.

Whether a romance was budding or not, Mrs Pimsleur came out to Constable Cheswick at noon with sandwiches and asked him how he has getting along?

"Very well, thank you, Mrs Pimsleur. Except for finding clues, of course. There are none out here to be found, I'm afraid." Constable Cheswick said.

Mrs Pimsleur nodded politely and set the tray of sandwiches on a table one of the servants had brought.

"Caleb," she said, suddenly using his familiar name, "Your mother and I were very good friends when I first came to Westwich, and she very kind to me. She would have been very proud to know you were studying botany." Mrs Pimsleur said.

"Thank you." Caleb Cheswick said. "I think I study it for my own interests, but I also think she may have influence over me yet."

"She would not be a bad influence to have, in that case." Laura Pimsleur smiled.

"Mrs Pimsleur, you have a dog, don't you? A big setter? Did it make any noise last night?"

"No. None that I know of." she turned to the servant standing by, "Haymitch? Did Cleve make any fuss last night?"

"No ma'am. Nothing I heard or any has mentioned." Haymitch (apparently) said.

Mrs Pimsleur turned her eyes back to Constable Cheswick, who merely shrugged.

"Wrong trail again, I suppose." he said.

***

The afternoon after his exhaustive investigation of the Pimsleur residence, Constable Cheswick put down on paper his official report to the district to inform them of the progress of his investigation as well as the new information which would compel them to send someone down to take over the case. In their third edition, Messrs Greene and Finchley set forth a template for official reports which Constable Cheswick now followed to the letter:

OFFICIAL REPORT of CRIMES COMMITTED in WESTWICH and SURROUNDING NEIGHBORHOOD.

(Write the date or dates of the crime or crimes committed or thought to have been committed. Be sure that the crime you are claiming has happened has really happened:)
DATES: Beginning April 21st and Ending May 2nd.

(Indicate the crime committed. If more than one crime is to be included in the report, specifically state each crime and the order in which they occurred- do this in a list for the ease of reading by superiors:)
LIST of CRIMES:
Robbery (first)
Robbery (second)
Robbery (third)
Robbery (fourth)
Robbery (fifth)

(Enumerate these:)
LIST of CRIMES:
1. Robbery (first)
2. Robbery (second)
3. Robbery (third)
4. Robbery (fourth)
5. Robbery (fifth)

(Include in your list these primary details:)

a) for murder: notate the number of victims
b) for robbery: notate the value in question for each incident
c) for arson: notate the number of buildings, indicating whether damaged or singed

LIST of CRIMES:
1. Robbery (first)
    a) none
    b) £14
    c) none, neither
2. Robbery (second)
    a) none
    b) £56
    c) none, neither
3. Robbery (third)
    a) none
    b) £78
    c) none, neither
4. Robbery (fourth)
    a) none
    b) £139
    c) none, neither
5. Robbery (fifth)
    a) none
    b) £100
    c) none, neither

(Be sure to include the address or approximate location of the crime.)
LIST of CRIMES:
1. Robbery (first) Blankenship home, East of Moor.

- a) none
- b) £14
- c) none, neither

2. Robbery (second) Harold home, East of Moor.
- a) none
- b) £56
- c) none, neither

3. Robbery (third) Rampert home (Huffington-In-Box), southeast of Moor.
- a) none
- b) £78
- c) none, neither

4. Robbery (fourth) Williams residence, Westwich Crossroads
- a) none
- b) £139
- c) none, neither

5. Robbery (fifth) Pimsleur home, south of Moor
- a) none
- b) £100
- c) none, neither

(Now you have given your superiors a general overlay of the crime(s) which they may refer to at a glance. Next, give a brief, descriptive narrative of the crime(s). Your description should follow the general timeline as you go and should include as little speculation as possible. Your superiors must have facts at their disposal. It will not do to sublimate the facts for personal grandiosity. Include transcripts of interviews at the end of the

report and footnote them appropriately- DO NOT include them here.)

1. Robbery (first) Blankenship home, East of Moor.
On the night of 21 April, 1803 Mr Blankenship (see interview 1a) reports a personal family heirloom, valuing approx. £14 was missing from his library. The Constable on Duty (Mr Caleb Cheswick) was summoned and inspected the crime scene that evening. The Constable on Duty also interviewed Mr Blankenship at this time (see interview 1a) and Mrs Blankenship (see interview 1b) both of whom indicated they had been on the premises- in the backyard of the house with guests- when the items appear to have been taken. Nothing more is known at this time and there are no suspects.

2. Robbery (second) Harold home, East of Moor.
On the night of 24 April, 1803 Mr Harold (see interview 2) reports an undisclosed personal item, valuing approx. £56 was missing from his personal effects. The Constable on Duty (Mr Caleb Cheswick) was summoned the following morning and inspected the crime scene promptly. The Constable on Duty also interviewed Mr Harold at this time (see interview 2a) and Mr Crick, a groundskeeper, (see interview 2b) both of whom indicated Mr Harold had been in town when the items appear to have been taken. Mr Harold himself was initially implicated but the charges were not brought before he was acquitted by a third

witness (see interview 2c). Nothing more is known at this time and there are no suspects.

3. Robbery (third) Huffington-In-Box home, southeast of Moor.
Notes not found. More is known and will be included in the report when those notes are found. I do remember that there are no suspects.

4. Robbery (fourth) Williams residence, Westwich Crossroads.
On the morning of 1 May, 1803 Miss Williams reports a pair of silver candlesticks, valued approx. £139 were missing from her dining room. The Constable on Duty (Mr Caleb Cheswick) was summoned that morning and inspected the crime scene promptly. The Constable on Duty also interviewed Miss Williams (see interview 4) and ascertained no more information. These are very expensive candlesticks. Nothing more is known at this time and there are no suspects.

5. Robbery (fifth) Pimsleur home, south of Moor.
On the night of 2 May, 1803 Mr Pimsleur (see interview 5a) reports personal effects; a watch and cufflinks, valuing approx. £100 was missing from his room. The Constable on Duty (Mr Caleb Cheswick) was summoned and inspected the crime scene that evening. The Constable on Duty also interviewed Mr Pimsleur at this time (see interview 5a) who indicated

he and his family had been out at Mrs B's dancing when the items appear to have been taken. The Constable on Duty spoke again with Mr Pimsleur the following morning and proceeded to inspect the grounds, doors and windows of the home. No transcript of an interview with any other specific family member is available at this time as there was no interview with any other specific family member. The Constable on Duty does intend to follow up on any leads and, if possible, conduct more interviews in this household. Nothing more is known at this time and there are no suspects.

(Your report should end with a summary, including all needed resources.)
SUMMARY
The present Constable on Duty is *constabule pro tempore* and untrained for this duty. Further, the sum total of losses incurred by the five crimes now exceeds the localized limit of jurisdiction. Assistance requested.
END of REPORT

Constable Caleb Cheswick made three copies (in five tries) of this report, packaged it with the transcripts of his interviews and sent it by highest priority to the district.

3 A RIDE IN THE NEIGHBOURHOOD

Mssrs Greene and Finchley instruct the observing investigator, once the preliminaries are done and the official investigation commenced, to tell the victims of the crime to proceed with their normal lives and routines while, of course, heightening their caution of any suspicious persons or activities. This allows for the victim to move on with their daily life and not giving the criminal the satisfaction of dominance by terror.

Thus, Constable Cheswick, whose mother had been friends with Mrs Pimsleur years ago, spoke to Fenton and Laura Pimsleur, "I would like to encourage you to proceed with your normal lives and routines," he read, "while, of course, heightening your sense of any suspicious persons or activities. This will allow you to move on with your daily life and not give the criminal the satisfaction of dominance by terror."

Constable Cheswick then requested permission to begin writing his report to the district right away, in fact, if he might have use of the study? To which they replied he might. So, while Constable Caleb Cheswick labored over his report to the district, the Pimsleur household was still learning to live life in a post-crime world. Normalcy, Mr Pimsleur said, was the key to the thing- by which, we assume he meant normalcy was the key to normalcy.

"Perhaps we may have more to give thanks for in our prayers; but all in all, life should go on as usual." Mr Pimsleur said.

His daughters, Hildegard and Penelope had been in close discussion about the merits of an afternoon walk and the safety of which when Mr Pimsleur, on the advice of the constable, had made his declarations regarding normalcy and keys. This declaration from Mr Pimsleur quickly swayed them to agreement in taking a walk about the neighborhood. Had Mr Pimsleur known his own power of influence in that moment and if he had any hint then of what he later found out, he would have said the key to normalcy would be to lock his daughters up in their rooms, bar the doors and have his gun at the ready. But we must all make decisions with the information we have. So the girls had decided to walk.

Thus it was that afternoon, Hildegard and Penelope put on their hats and laced up their boots for perambulations. The pending withdrawal of the two young ladies to the outdoors suited Mr Pimsleur just fine because his own personal key to normalcy was to take a nice, long nap and all the better if the house was quiet. Things were going smoothly until, in addition to these keys to normalcy, Mrs Pimsleur suggested the girls might be helpful in delivering invitations to a forthcoming dinner whilst on their walk and her daughters happily agreed to these terms of helpfulness.

Mrs Pimsleur's keys to normalcy were as carefully selected as the china in the cabinet and the linen on the table and were curated along a theme resembling denial cloaked in practical manners. This isn't to say Mrs Pimsleur herself was in denial. She believed instead that she should be the one to carry the burden to let the girls carry on their own days in peace. How she handled this, privately, while the her husband slept and the girls were out would not be known to the rest of the family for many years (when a saucy housekeeper's maid had decided she had had enough and played the only card she carried) and does not come into this story at all.

Nevertheless, Mrs Pimsleur's request carried with it the necessity of waiting for a horse and phaeton to be prepared; which required the finding of the groom, which didn't take nearly as long as finding someone to find him since he had been in the kitchen finishing off the sandwiches from Cheswick's lunch, and when it was done the girls were ready to be home and were not looking forward to the ride after all. So, with all the good intentions of the respective family members, the sisters' path through the neighborhood was already paved in an ominous direction.

As they rode along, the sisters poured forth their respective emotions regarding the previous night's break-in and burglary in a manner befitting two sisters who are also best friends and as the time went on, they found themselves more and more at ease about things and also more and more absorbed in their conversation than in their surroundings. This mode of distraction was at that very moment being taken advantage of by a shadowy figure several hundred steps behind them. This dark clad follower stayed to the one side of the road, advantageously navigating the shadows of overhanging trees and occasionally stepping off the road completely if one of the two sisters appeared to hesitate or turned her head more than necessary.

Penelope, it should be noted here in regards to danger and burglars, had organised a series of societies as a child- to which only she and her sister were available or allowed to join- in order to sniff out the dangerous and preposterous ideas in her head regarding Ghosts, Conspiracies, and Criminals-In-Hiding. This last category of the underworld, Criminals-In-Hiding, had three separate societies all its own over the course of a single autumn. Now, as a near-adult, she was known still to read half-penny novels with such discouraging titles as, *The Icy Blue Hand of Death Which Strangles People,* and *The Regrettable Diversions of the Reclusive Ms Puccini,* and *A Day in*

Sommersville. Suffice to say, she was a young woman who was easy to excite, but difficult to shock.

If either of the young women had turned around, it is hard to say whether they would have even noticed anyone following them- but if she had turned around at just the right moment to see a glimpse of a shadow melting into the trees, then their terror would have been full of the unknown designs of such a strange and sinister mode of behavior.

This scenario presents a difficulty to the reader and the difficulty is this: do we want the girls to turn around and discover their pursuer or do we want them to blissfully enjoy their ride? If they discover the truth of their situation, what would they do? Might they in fact react in a way that enhances their danger? Perhaps they would attempt to make a getaway or turn the phaeton around and speed past the shadowy figure- this could end in disaster! But if the girls do not discover they are being followed, then they could be in danger at every turn, and may be set upon without warning.

This predicament is enhanced by our pursuer's unknown intent. Does this shadow mean them harm? Or merely to observe them? Both are unpleasant thoughts but at least they may not be in immediate danger and that is a relief if we let ourselves believe they are only being observed.

Their danger would perhaps be made clear very soon, as the girls approached the first house in the neighborhood. The property they came to and turned up the driveway (the gate there was less elaborate than their own and not at all famous) was once the summer home of Lord Huffington-In-Box and still referred to in that day as Huffington-in-Box. It belonged now to Mr Rampert and living in the former residence of gentility suited him just fine. The story had been that many years ago Lord Huffington had come into some hard financial times for reasons which were too personal to disclose to the general public and had sold the property for pence on the pound to Mr Rampert at the height of his modest wealth- nearly all of which he spent on the estate. Lord Huffington then seemingly disappeared from the face of the earth. Local talk at the time had been that he went to the Indias with all that was left of his money but in time, his disappearance from the face of the earth became the preferred way of telling the story.

The only stipulation of the Huffington-In-Box deal, apparently, had been that the cottage in the south parts of the property be retained, intact, and left entirely alone. The eccentricities of cash-strapped nobility notwithstanding, the cottage was left well alone and if Lord Huffington, in fact, had corporeally disappeared from the face of the earth and still haunted there in the summers it was without Mr Rampert's direct knowledge.

Mr Rampert suffered from a chronic condition and received the girls with much coughing and complaining and coughed on the invitation and coughed on the bureau looking for his handkerchief and after a brief interval of calm in which he formally accepted the invitation, coughed again. The girls, being inclined to leave him to it, were then subjected to an abnormally early tea and much coughing whilst Mr Rampert, delighted to have female companionship, began telling them the story of the burglary which had occurred at his home only a few weeks earlier.

"I was kkhaaw in the gar- kkhaawwl garden all hhhwwkk hhhwwwkk khaaaaaak day." He said. "I was in ghaaak in the garden. Hck hck. I was in the garden."

And so on.

The girls' patience, being nearly infinite, did not run out before the tea did and they were permitted to extricate themselves from the premises on the grounds they had other invitations to deliver and they were graciously led to the door by a manservant, Mr Rampert's hacking and coughing in the parlor receding as they left. The sister's never learned what actually happened on that fateful day Mr Rampert was burgled, but they knew with certainty he had been in the garden.

This brief respite brings us back to our difficulty, as the girls return to their phaeton and their ride through the neighborhood, the individual who is following them remains at large. But thankfully they arrived at Mrs B's home without incident.

Mrs B was not available- being out on the grounds (perhaps in her own garden) and the girls could not wait for her to be fetched and as it was not necessary anyway, they left. But the invitation was delivered and the girls resumed.

"Pen?" Hildegard said.

"Yes, Hilde?" Penelope said.

"Pen, tea with Mr Rampert took an awfully long time, dear. We may have time for one more stop but we should really be turning ourselves around for home."

"Darling, I think we could make two stops if we hurry. Mama would be pleased, wouldn't she, if we could deliver all the invitations?"

"Pen, dearest, it is getting late."

"My beloved Hilde, our phaeton could deliver three more invitations and get us home before dark."

"I know you are right, dear, it is only your safety I am thinking of."

"Darling, I also am always thinking of your safety with no break in my affections for you. And in the light of my concern for you i see quite clearly that there is no danger of not finishing our little task in time."

"Well, then let us finish out little task, dear. But we must hurry straight home after."

"Of course."

This exchange amounted to a pitched battle between the two and when the girls returned home, they reported to their parents the argument in even more subdued terms than it had actually amounted to, though they called it, "Quite the peck and paw, Mama!"

In the meantime, the girls were still out on the road and being followed by a shadowy figure as the dusk drew near, closing them in even as the golden hour began. Had they known their road back home was blocked by a stranger, I still don't know what they would have done. In the end, though, they were rescued by none other than Constable Caleb Cheswick.

As the girls had finished their last invitation delivery of the day, they returned to the little carriage and made for the road once more, this time they intended to turn to the right for home. But at the end of the drive, there stood a solitary figure in a long, dark overcoat. As they girls approached, he seemed to have no intention of acknowledging their presence, when he suddenly jumped to attention. The girls did not know him.

"Misses Pimsleur!" He said.

"Oh, Constable Cheswick." The girls said, recognizing him finally, as if he had not already been at their house all morning and as if their mama had not brought lunch out to him. "How do you do?"

"I am well, thank you. And you?" He said, as if he had not already been at their house all morning and even ate lunch there.

"Very well, thank you, Constable." The girls both said at the same time.

"And you, Miss Penelope, how are you?" he said.

"Very well, thank you, Constable." Penelope said, repeating herself.

"I am very glad to hear it, Misses. I must trouble you- although I hope it is no trouble to you and I certainly don't mean it to be troubling- but have you by chance seen anyone out today on the road? Perhaps someone, hrm, behind you on the road today?"

"Why, no, Constable. There was no person on the road with us today." Hildegard said innocently.

"I don't mean *with* you, Ms Hildegard. I ask again; did you notice anyone *behind* you. Perhaps someone following you?"

The girls started at this insinuation that someone may have been following them. "Goodness, no!" they said as one. The exclamation with which they said this was sufficient to ease Cheswick's immediate concern.

"I am glad to hear this, too." He said. Then he turned more serious. "Misses Pimsleur. I must inform you that as I began my evening rounds, I spied an individual on the road. This individual seemed to have a particular interest in your excursion today and so I followed this person. Somewhere between Huffington and here, however, the individual seems to have left the road entirely and slipped into the field on one side or the other."

This was most alarming to the girls, but they were very glad for Constable Cheswick's observance and care of them and told him so.

"No, no, Misses, I am the Constable here. Even if I am *Constable Pro Tempore*, I will continue to fulfill my duties to the utmost wherever our citizens are concerned." this he said looking mainly in the direction of Hildegard, but by his determination not to look her way when he said it, most certainly meant Penelope when he said 'citizens'.

"By your gracious leave, I will accompany you back to your home. I must be certain that you are safe from anyone out here on the road." he said.

The girls could not refuse the officer of the law but since there was no more room in the two-seater phaeton, he was obligated to walk alongside them. This, of course, meant they arrived home much later than they would have otherwise, but they did arrive safely home and without incident.

Constable Caleb Cheswick reported to Mr Pimsleur his observations of the strange follower on the road and cautioned him to incorporate more caution into his normal routine.

"I thought at first he might be another botany enthusiast. He seemed to dart back and forth and bend and crouch as if in examination. Then I noticed the young ladies in their carriage and I began to suspect something wrong. Perhaps the young ladies should be accompanied whenever they leave the premises?" young Cheswick suggested.

"Yes, yes. I'll think that over Constable. I will be sure someone is responsible for them at all times." Mr Pimsleur said.

"As an officer of the law, Mr Pimsleur, I am a servant of the community." Constable Cheswick offered.

"Thank you, Constable. I'm sure I or one my manservants will be with them at all times from now on." Mr Pimsleur said.

As the young and inexperienced temporary constable retreated down the steps of the Pimsleur home, Mr Pimsleur found himself a little relieved that very soon there would be a real professional in charge of the investigation. Did that mean there would a new Constable, too? Mr Pimsleur made himself a note to ask about that.

"Well, he will make a fine botanist someday." he told his wife, "Provided he finds a little ambition along the way."

4 "SOMETHING OUGHT TO BE DONE"

In Which it is Discovered Something Has Already Been Done.

For the sake of clarity, we must pause now to describe the place and situation in which our story takes place. At the crossroads, years ago, a small inn, a pub and a post station had blossomed into the small hamlet of Westwich, which eventually became the societal and cultural hub of the county- though having no competition in that respect it had certainly taken its time. Buildings and structures progressed slowly in each of the four directions of the crossroad and Westwich proper was formed. But as time went on, the more affluent of the hamlet began building homes to the east and to the south, more and more. This development was strange because that was the direction of the heath, which lay directly southeast of

Westwich. Thus, along the north end of the heath, and the west edge of the heath, homes and estates were established, paths became roads, homes and estates became larger and larger, until eventually the entire heath was ringed in by this unusual extension of the town.

The crossroad itself, however, did not become what it was expected to be. Since a crossroad is comprised, usually, of two intersecting roads, let us examine each. The road running, approximately, north to south was a busy one until a better one was built further to the west, along with a more direct route and a better bridge, and the one running through Westwich fell out of popularity. Now the north-south road went south to Brakton, where there was a proper train station and north to, well, not much of anywhere useful.

So, the saving grace of Westwich's usefulness to the Empire was left to its connection from the new north-south road (to the west) to the budding seaport town, Westhead, to the east, about twelve miles away on the coast. Westwich lay on the most direct route from Westhead to the main north-south road. This route from Westhead on the sea to the now-better north-south road would still put Westwich in the midst of the commerce action, so to speak.

Westhead was built on cargo and commerce-goods being shipped up the coast by boat from London. This was all well and good but the harbor at Westhead was one of limited depth, and soon larger ships were being built and replacing the smaller ships with shallower drafts- larger ships which no could no longer enter the Westhead harbor except at high tide. This meant all the warehouses, inns and pubs built to support the budding shipping industry dried up within a few years and became a place where one could occasionally get a decent pint but not much else. So the (now, relatively speaking) useless seaport of Westhead become colloquially known as Wasted.

So the rise and fall of Westwich as a player in the larger world was swift enough to bring a town together but not so dramatic as to ruin it.

The Pimsleurs lived on the very south of the heath in one of the largest estates and nearly the furthest from Westwich proper. Here on the south side of the heath, the distance between homes was as far as the distance from one end to the other of Westwich proper. Penelope and Hildegard Pimsleur had narrowly avoided tragedy on this southerly road of the heath while they delivered their mother's invitations. A stranger had been following them in secret and word spread quickly through the area about this sinister scenario. Concerned citizens of Westwich had called a town meeting and two nights later, nearly the whole town was sat in the church.

This little church could hold nearly half the residents of Westwich in its pews- which tells us more about the population of Westwich than the size of the church, but since this church was out on the North road of the moor, it was a church which really only the class of families which lived around the moor attended- those with estates and carriages of their own, and little need of a church which served the needs of the common town folk. It was located directly on the North Road (this is the road which ran from Wasted to the new north-south road) with frontage right along the lane, and on the property of the Blankenship family- two siblings, a brother and sister, who lived together- whose money had built the church originally and kept themselves responsible for maintaining the salary of the rector and a strict litigation on membership to the parochial council.

The rector, in this case, was a Father Leamas whose religious affiliations were, of course, with the Anglican Archdiocese but who still privately held to some of the catholic ideas- which, truth be told, was perfectly fine with the Bishop at York- and maintained the custom of being referred to as 'father', citing St Paul's first letter to the Corinthians regarding an abundance of teachers and a dearth of fathers.

Miss Blankenship, the sister, had commandeered a gavel in the very early stages of the meeting and seemed to be running things from the pulpit. Mr Blankenship, the brother, stood a little to her left and made motions for quiet which looked as if he were patting children on their heads. Constable Cheswick sat in the front row. The Pimsleurs and other victims of the recent robberies were given seats near the front as though they were guests of honor. The rest of the audience filled the remaining pews and stood about at the back. It was very hot in the hall (most of the town had shown up uninvited and it was not built or properly ventilated for so many) and throughout the meeting windows were opened and closed intermittently. When the temperature rose and it became too stuffy, someone would call for windows to be opened. When the windows were opened, a terrific cross-breeze would manifest itself upon the ladies' hats and someone would call for the windows to be closed. This went on until Ms Blankenship gaveled several times on the pulpit and declared no windows could be opened or closed without permission from the chair- meaning, herself.

The Blankenship siblings' estate was modest by comparison to those on the south side, but theirs was where the priory was, and from thence it was assumed came Miss Blankenship's authority to call such a meeting. We should say here that if our story required a villainess, we would vote for Miss Blankenship to play the role.

"Of the five robberies which were recently committed in Westwich, four of them have come about the heath." Miss Blankenship was saying. "The chair requests those victims of the robberies to provide their thoughts and feelings about the crimes and to give us their opinion whether enough is being done to curb the rampant felonies."

At the word, 'felonies', Constable Cheswick raised his hand to correct her misuse of the word but her brother patted an imaginary head in the

Constable's direction and Ms Blankenship went on without a beat.

"We will proceed clockwise." she said. "The chair calls for Mr Blankenship."

The siblings exchanged places- but the expression of their face was one and the same.

"Thank you." he said. "On the evening of April 21st, as we dined with Father Leamas, a criminal broke into and entered our house, our home, our fortress, and took from our very lives a precious family heirloom. A broach. A broach was stolen from our very souls!"

Even Father Leamas, known for his repetitive rhetoric, thought this was a bit much.

"The esteemed Blankenship estate," Mr Blankenship said, meaning he and his sister. "Demands an explanation from the Constable, the defender of the law, the deputised champion of justice! As to what his actions have been, what his intentions are. What will he do to curtail this crime wave that threatens all of us!"

Constable Cheswick rose to answer but Ms Blankenship was too quick for him. She quickly reached across her brother and gaveled until the Constable sat down again. Mr Blankenship continued.

"It is the responsbility of the Constable to maintain order and peace in our fair hamlet." he said.

Mr Pimsleur now raised his hand, taking exception to the burden being laid solely on the

"Something Ought To Be Done."

novice shoulders of the young *Constabule Pro Tempore*. "We the citizens of Westwich," he said.

"The chair does not recognise interruptions from the floor during testimony!" Ms Blankenship said and gaveled a clean new dent in the pulpit.

Mr Blankenship liked the term, though, and adopted it as his own. "We the citizens of Westwich say- nay, we demand! Something must be done!"

We are sorry to say there was much cheering of this statement. Constable Cheswick raised his hand, hoping to be acknowledged. Whether 'the chair' noticed him or not, Mr Rampert now came to the pulpit in the midst of the cheering and Mr Blankenship could think of nothing else to say at that precise moment. Several voices called for Mr Rampert to speak and give his own testimony. Mr Rampert, of course, was another recent victim of robbery.

Ms. Blankenship leapt in and gaveled. "The chair calls Mr. Rampert!" she said, though Mr Rampert was already halfway up the stairs. The Pimsleur girls, who had tea with Mr Rempert only that week had been anxious to know what happened that day, leaned forward in their seats from the second row. He appeared solemn, and his eyes looked over the crowd, then he looked again. Then he appeared surprised to still have the attention of anyone in the room. It took several moments to gather himself during which he appeared to be deciding whether he should continue or not. He began his testimony.

"I was kkhaaw in the gar- kkhaawwl garden all hhhwwkk hhhwwwkk khaaaaaak day." He coughed. "I was in ghaaak in the garden. Hck hck. I was in the garden."

That was enough for them. Ms Blankenship gaveled like beaten copper while Mr Blankenship escorted Mr Rampert back to his seat. The Pimsleur girls sighed and sat back in their own seats, no wiser than before.

A booming voice from somewhere in the back and to the left of the crowd could not be ignored. "When are we going to talk about the post tax? I myself might start thieving if the post tax is increased again!"

More cheering. More gaveling.

"The post tax is necessary, Mr Silverstonne, but does not come into the purview of this meeting. We are discussing crimes which have been committed already." Mr Blankenship said.

"The post tax IS a crime!" Mr Silverstonne said. He did not sit down. He simply stood there.

"We are not discussing the legality of the post tax, sir." Miss Blankenship was at her end. "Father Leamas, kindly ask your parishioner to be seated and observe the rules of decorum." she said.

"I'm not his parishioner!" Mr Silverstonne said. It was true; this was his first time in the church since moving to Westwich. "I'm a parishioner of Lettingham!"

Ms Blankenship had her opening.

"Then, Mr Silverstonne, I must ask you to be seated. Non-parishioners must keep silent." she said. "I believe the Holy Word is clear on that, at least." She nodded to Father Leamas, who did his best not to acknowledge what she had said but somehow appear supportive of the general proceeding while Mr Silverstonne sat down, being unable to stand against the dual testimony of both the Holy Word and the rules of decorum.

Young Caleb Cheswick stood up to get the attention of Ms Blankenship so he might address the issue at hand, but someone called out,

"What about the vagrant hooligan?", echoed by others. More gaveling.

"What vagrant hooligan, the Chair would like to know?" said Miss Blankenship.

"The vagrant hooligan who's been skulking about town the last couple weeks!" the voice said. It may have belonged to the pub owner.

"Has anyone else seen this vagrant hooligan?" Miss Blankenship said.

Several nods and a few "Aye!" were heard.

"We will bring this up at the proper moment. In the meantime, the Chair calls Ms Williams!" Miss Blankenship said.

Ms Williams, accompanied by Father Leamas, now came to the pulpit to stand as a troubled brook between two pillars of a distant bridge, the Blankenship siblings standing one on either side of her. Father Leamas, having deposited her, returned to his seat.

"Now, Ms Williams, how do you feel about the robbery which took place in your home and took from you not only priceless belongings but also your own personal security?" Mr Blankenship said.

"Well, the candlesticks weren't priceless- they, were, expensive. But I wouldn't quite say they were priceless."

"Ms Williams, no one can put a price on such family heirlooms." Miss Blankenship insisted.

"Oh, I bought them last winter for myself. They're not heirlooms. I bought them in Westhead at Mr Gimberley's shop." Ms Williams explained.

She would never know it, but Ms Blankenship was getting a first-rate education in the importance of fact-checking.

"Surely, Ms Williams, they would have been heirlooms handed down to your children and your children's children and to their children?" Miss Blankenship said.

"Yes, I suppose. One of them had already been chipped- I don't have any children who would be interested in them." Ms WIlliams said.

"And how do you feel about Constable Cheswick's handling of your unfortunate situation? Are you concerned that he has not yet apprehended the thief?" Miss Blankenship said.

"No. I think he is a very smart young man and will certainly do his duty the best he can." Ms

Williams said, softly as a lamb.

Ms Williams was gaveled and Mr Blankenship escorted her halfway down the stair until handing her off to Father Leamas.

"The chair calls Mr Harold."

There was no movement in the crowd.

"The chair calls Mr Harold!" louder this time.

Still no movement in the crowd.

"He's out! Not here!" someone said.

Miss Blankenship gaveled. Mostly in frustration.

"The chair calls Mr Pimsleur." she finally said.

Mr Fenton Pimsleur rose and side stepped his way through to the aisle. The Blankenship siblings waited patiently for him to approach- his estate was bigger than theirs, after all. Fenton Pimsleur did not take the pulpit straight on but stood a little to the right of it. The gathering seemed to settle when he stood before them.

"Young Mr Caleb Cheswick is doing a fine job and is doing, in my opinion, all that can be done in his position- is being done." Mr Pimsleur said. "I have no doubt this thief will be apprehended and this crime spree-" Here he looked pointedly at Mr Blankenship. "This crime spree will be at an end."

A general applause rippled through the crowd. He continued.

"Mr Silverstonne, do you know what the post tax pays for?"

"Excuse me, Mr Pimsleur, that is beyond the purview of this meeting. We must stay to the topic at hand, which is this crime, uh, wave, and what needs to be done about it. Do you have anything to add to the discussion?"

"I would like to hear some more about this vagrant hooligan. Could we have a description please?" Mr Pimsleur said.

Many voices at once were gaveled down and sorted into an audio queue. When it was all said and done, Constable Cheswick- who had been listening attentively with a pen and pad- had a reasonably consistent description of a unknown man in shabby clothing, unkempt, tall and lanky (whether he truly had beady eyes would remain to be seen) and seen in various locations a few weeks ago- but now no one could remember properly seeing him since. It was possible this vagrant hooligan was, in fact, the thief they were looking for and now he was in hiding.

"This sounds like something that should have been brought to the Constable's attention weeks ago. I trust he will pursue this avenue of investigation now though, eh? (Constable Cheswick nodded solemnly) Beyond that, I don't think there is anything else that needs to be said. All that can be done is being done." Mr Pimsleur said.

When Pimsleur had sat down with his family, Mr Blankenship resumed. "We all can agree, I think, without reservation that all that can be done is being done. The question before is whether something ought to be done."

"Something Ought To Be Done."

Mr Pimsleur stood again, risking the ire of the Blankenships and asked whether the constable might be allowed to speak? No cornered animal could look as fierce as Ms Blankenship did in that moment. But she smiled. And gaveled.

"The chair calls Constable Caleb Cheswick." She said his name as if there might have been other constables in the room and it was necessary to distinguish between them all.

The Blankenship siblings did not move as the young constable came up the stairs. He stopped at the top step and turned around. Then he thought better of facing so many people at once and turned halfway back to the pulpit and faced it, directly addressing it when he spoke. He pulled a paper from his pocket and unfolded it. To his great and unexpected credit, most of the audience heard him when he read aloud the following telegram.

"From District Office. Stop. Have rcvd your crime report. Stop. Expect Inspector Foxglove arrival soon."

Only the most perceptive person in the room would have noticed just a little smile on the face of Penelope Pimsleur when Cheswick had finished reading this news. "Well, clearly something HAS been done. And Mr Caleb Cheswick has done it." she thought proudly to herself, and then a moment later suddenly wondered why she felt pride, of all things?

The general atmosphere of the room switched very quickly after the reading of the telegram response. Once united in agitation and eschewing common sense as if they were one entity, the people gathered in the chapel that evening become docile and quiet. The gavel came down again and the meeting was quickly adjourned. Miss Blankenship did not thank anyone for coming.

5 THE APPEARANCE OF FOXGLOVE

In Which We Have Our First Look at the Master Detective at Work.

Two days passed after Constable Cheswick had sent his official report. On the third afternoon he received a telegram response from the district regarding his report and the arrival of an individual named, Inspector Foxglove. He had brought this message to the town meeting in hopes of reading it at the first and avoiding the rest of what he had correctly anticipated being a disastrous meeting. This instinct being accurate, as we witnessed borne out in the previous chapter.. Afterward he felt he might have saved the Blankenships some trouble, and possibly a little embarrassment, by reading it but no opportunity had been afforded him to do so. It is often those who we might help the most who receive it the least.

Despite the message, though, he was not expecting the doorknock.

He was sitting at his desk in the constabulary office, which was on the main street of Westwich, next to the *Bear and Ox* public house when he heard a knock on the door. Before he could stand up, the same door had opened and in walked a striking and altogether admirable figure he had never seen before. He was tall, broad-shouldered and clearly an able man. The man had swept into the room as if he expected action and he looked as though he might catch anything thrown at him.

The bold stranger had a prepossession, an attitude, which immediately both set one at ease and put one on one's best behavior. Cheswick found himself immediately filled with the desire to impress this man and yet it was clear no one really could impress such an impressive man. His quick eyes, his bearing, and his capable hands spoke to a military background. His manner was that of learned and scholarly man. His smile was that of a princely host. His voice commanded respect and quick ears. He crossed the large room in two might strides, his boots all thunder, and introduced himself.

"Good afternoon. I am Inspector Foxglove. You are Constable Cheswick, I presume?" the man said.

Cheswick was clearly startled by the appearance of the venerable inspector so soon after the telegram and despite his best intentions, could not pull himself together.

"You are early sir. If I may?" He said.

Foxglove bowed as he pulled off his riding gloves. He extended his hand and Cheswick shook it.

There was a brief silence.

Cheswick gathered himself and spoke.

"Inspector Foxglove, I am certainly honored and relieved to have you here. As you know I am only the constable here on a *pro tempore* basis, filling in for my recently passed father. I'm sure you have seen such circumstances before, where an old tradition puts a novice in a position of authority until common sense may prevail. I hope you can quickly solve this case and I am hoping I may, in fact, leave as soon as possible. I have university, you see, and am already far, far behind on my studies there." he said.

Inspector Foxglove shook his head in a way Cheswick knew there was no arguing it, "I'm afraid that will be impossible, Constable. I am only here for this specific case, or, serial of cases. I have no jurisdiction or authority to replace or even to find a replacement. That will all come from the district but not by my hand. No. You will need to stay here for some time, I imagine. In the meantime, though, you may set your mind at ease about the case at hand. I am in charge of it now. What we need to do next is to have a proper transfer of the case. You will need to provide me with all your reports, investigative notes, procedural annotations and interview transcripts."

"Did you not receive all that already, Inspector? I sent it all by post." Cheswick said.

"I like to have it all first hand, Constable. I do not like loose ends and I certainly don't like assumptions." Foxglove said, his eyebrows implying that Cheswick had already made a grievous mistake in assumption. He must have betrayed this internal feeling on his outward features, since Foxglove smiled suddenly.

"I am no taskmaster, Constable. I am firm, but you and I are both on the right side of the law. It is our duty and our privilege to bring justice and I relish the opportunity to bring justice to the victims of this heinous crime. Secretly, between you and me, I am delighted to be here doing my own special work."

This last statement seemed to put Constable Cheswick very much at ease.

"Now, Constable, I need dinner. I shall go have some next door (the *Bear and Ox*, is it?) while you gather your investigative material. Bring it along as quick as you can- I need to know all you know about this quaint town, it's people, it's country, the case and it's victims. You will be doing a lot of talking, I warn you: and I will keep you hydrated!" he said.

With that, Inspector Foxglove left the office as if raptured through the doorway.

When Cheswick finally arrived next door with the case notes, he found a small crowd gathered, and the unmistakable figure of Inspector Foxglove seated in the center. Foxglove was speaking in grave tones and everyone gathered around him was hushed and reverent. He appeared to be relaying some important information to the small crowd. Cheswick had just closed the door of the pub quietly as a mouse behind him when he overheard Foxglove fairly shout in a francophone accent, "So the farmer says, 'Asparagus?! I thought this was celery!'" And the crowd erupted in laughter! What Cheswick had taken for serious talk had only been a long and complicated joke.

When he saw Cheswick, Inspector Foxglove rose courteously and said to the rest, "Now please excuse us, your esteemed Constable and I have business to attend to. Please give us a little space. Thank you, thank you!"

There followed then several minutes as nearly everyone had to shake the Inspector's hand and offer a word of some kind to him, whether of admiration or thanks or some quirk they felt was peculiar to them and were certain of which he would understand.

When the two officers of the law were finally seated alone and the meal brought to them, Foxglove remarked on the gathering he had created.

"You noticed, Constable, that I spend time with people not connected to the case. That is not merely good manners, consider, they may really be part of a case down the road. In which case I want to have a rapport already built with them, and not merely when it is convenient. The inconvenience (though it really isn't an inconvenience) saves me time down the line when it comes to doing the job right. It is necessary, young man, to cultivate a rapport with the people you serve. You must serve them in silence and behind the scenes and unthanked; but you must also be among them. The sheep must know the voice of the shepherd if they are to follow him, are they not?" Foxglove said.

"I hadn't thought of it like that, Inspector. I shall take good note of that." Cheswick said.

"You and I are sheepdogs, Constable. We are the Watchers. But we must also walk among them and strengthen them from within. You and I cannot end the violence of the world on our own- each of them must rise up and we must teach them how." Foxglove said.

"Inspector Foxglove, you expand my understanding of the world at every turn!" Cheswick said.

The meal came now and clearly Inspector Foxglove was used to the finest of meals; as dish after dish was brought out and spread before them. A second smaller table was brought to accommodate the extra dishes.

"The French have their Porthos- the English have me!" Foxglove smiled broadly at the feast and tucked in his napkin. "Now Constable, let's have your report."

For nearly two hours Caleb Cheswick read his notes, reports and interviews, word for word, to the Inspector and took intermittent draughts for his dry throat. When he finished, the Inspector began to question him about the victims of the crimes, asking

The Appearance of Foxglove

and inquiring deep into details he perceived the young Cheswick had never dreamed as being of any importance. His inquiries were things like this:

"How high did you say the windows were from the ground on the east side of the house?",

and,

"When Mr Harold told you where he had been, did you look at you directly or did he glance about?",

or,

"Does the Pimsleur family have a poor or excellent reputation in the neighborhood?",

And,

"Which day is the post most often late to arrive?"

And many other such questions, all of which Constable Cheswick was surprised to know the answers to already.

"You see, Constable, there is something of the investigator in your blood. You must make it a habit, then, to draw these details and sound out each one. To discover what each feather tells you about the whole bird. These details you took up without realising it, by the way, are just the kinds of details a thief would notice, and you noticed them- that is good! A good investigator thinks like a policeman- a great investigator thinks like the thief! Now, you must learn to trust those instincts and not push them aside." Foxglove said.

"You think I think like a thief, Inspector? I don't know what to say." Cheswick said.

"I'm sure you would never think of becoming a thief, Mr Cheswick. But let us return to the crimes, each in turn. Firstly, the Blankenships." Foxglove said, reading from his own notes now. "The items in question?"

"It was a broach." Cheswick said, "Valued at fourteen."

"And the Blankenships say they were home at the time?" Foxglove said.

"Yes. Father Leamas was there, having dinner with them. Erm, Father Leamas is the rector on the moor." Cheswick said.

"You say Father Leamas is the rector? Is that why he is called Father?" Foxglove said, finding it amusing Cheswick was explaining such things to him.

"That is precisely why." Cheswick said.

"What manner of persons are the Blankenships, Constable?" Foxglove said.

Cheswick looked around him before speaking, seemingly out of habit. "The Blankenships, sir, are siblings- a brother and sister. They are, um, respected in the neighborhood, I suppose; after a fashion. They built the rectory- or rather, their family did. And they still pay for the upkeep and for Father Leamas' income."

"They are very religious?" Foxglove said.

"I suppose that's the word." Cheswick said. "Although somehow it's never struck me as quite the right word to describe them.

"Interesting." Foxglove said. "Where is the rectory? And does Father Leamas live there or elsewhere?"

"Oh yes, he lives there. There is a proper living quarters- an entire house, really right next to the rectory. Well, it's all the rectory, isn't it?" Cheswick said.

"That's very kind of the Blankenships. I'm eager to meet them as they certainly seem like pillars of the community?" Foxglove's eyebrows questioned Cheswick.

"You asked what kind of people they are, Inspector. They are pillars, perhaps. More likely they are pillars which one shouldn't trust with too much weight." Cheswick said, hoping it was tactful.

"I see. They are unreliable?" Foxglove said.

"Trustworthiness would be found where it concerns them to be so. They are quite reliable when it benefits them." Cheswick said.

"Very good. I have a sense of how to approach such people." Foxglove said. He made a few scratches in his notebook.

"Let's see, ah, the Harold family. Tell me about the Harolds, Constable." Foxglove said.

Cheswick brightened at the opportunity to speak well of someone. "They are fine people, Inspector. One can always find them involved in one thing or another. They are good neighbors and are part of an extended family of some note, I hear." Cheswick said. "Mr Harold has a peculiar quirk which is his own special attribute, which I may say, I'm not sure is always correct."

"A strange quirk which is not always correct?" Foxglove said. "That sounds easy enough to deal with. What of the rest of their household?"

"They have a number of children, all ages. They have more geese than anyone else in the neighborhood." Cheswick said.

"Geese? Is that really relevant?" Foxglove said.

"It was a particular detail I noticed. You said details should be dug up, not buried?" Cheswick said.

"That is not the metaphor I used, I'm sure of it. But let me ask this- is it common knowledge in the community the Harolds have more geese than anyone, or is it a particular detail only you uncovered?" Foxglove said.

"I see your point, Inspector. It is common knowledge. Perhaps that is not the kind of detail which needs dug up?" Cheswick said.

"No, perhaps not." Foxglove said. "Now, Constable, do you have or do you not have your notes of your interview with Mr Rampert? I see a glaring lack of interview notes here."

"Ah, that is a difficult one. My notes of the interview, are, inconclusive." Cheswick said.

Foxglove's eyebrows asked a dozen questions.

"The interview consisted mainly of my questions and his coughing, sir." Cheswick said.

Cheswick had never known the interrogation of such eyebrows.

"Well, Constable, I think I know a thing or two about interviews. I will go myself and extract all the necessary information. I will also need some understanding of each of the crime scenes. I hope that you may accompany me this week and we will visit each of the victims and go over these interviews with each of them together. This is a critical research phase of the case and we must capture all we can as soon as we can before the victim's memories are gone forever. The interviews are difficult already since victims never actually know what happened to them- you see, Constable, interviews are merely an excuse for the wily investigator to be at the crime scene and take it in for himself. You will see things, hear things and even feel things no victim can comprehend. You will seem clairvoyant if you investigate in the mindset of the thief, rather than the mindset of a policeman- or, heaven forbid, the mindset of a victim!" Foxglove said.

Cheswick, never without his notebook, was writing furiously as Foxglove spoke. Foxglove eyed the book.

"Is that notebook always with you, Constable?" Foxglove said.

"It certainly is, Inspector. Except when I forget it at home or at the office." Cheswick said.

"You are a botanist, is that right, Constable?" Foxglove said.

"I am studying to be one, Inspector." Cheswick said.

"So you know the area well, is that right? Where all the unique plants are, as well as the usual local flora, I suppose?" Foxglove said.

"I certainly do. It is my speciality." said Cheswick.

"Then, *Constable Pro Tempore*, I may need your help more than I anticipated." Foxglove said. "Now tell me about the Miss Williams. Candlesticks, I believe?"

"That's right, candlesticks. She insists they are candelabras but, quite honestly, I think we just call them candlesticks." Cheswick said.

"Hmm?" Foxglove said.

"Candelabra- that's a French word, isn't it? I think we just call them candlesticks." Cheswick said.

"Is Miss Williams such a fancy person that she changes the words she uses?" Foxglove said.

"No, not at all. That is the odd thing-" Cheswick began.

"Constable, that is also not a detail you need to worry about." Foxglove said.

Cheswick nodded, and continued on another path.

"Miss Williams is a widow, her husband passed several years ago. No children that I know of." Cheswick said.

"And the Pimsleurs?" Foxglove said.

"Well, they have a daughter- two daughters. Miss Penelope and Miss Hildegard." Cheswick said.

Foxglove waited for him to continue.

"Is that all, Constable? They have two daughters? Is that all you wish to convey about a family whose house was broken into?" Foxglove said.

"Oh. The Pimsleurs- Mr Fenton and Mrs Pimsleur. Her name is Laura. They are a very special family in Westwich. Well-liked. Very well-respected. There has been some talk in the past about getting him appointed, Mr Pimsleur, to some kind of office of some kind. I don't really know what. But he would likely win, if they put it to a vote. Which, I suppose that isn't what they do in an appointment, anyway. They seem to get along with everyone. They have the biggest estate in the neighborhood." Cheswick said.

"Very good for them. Now Constable, do you have any suspects?" Foxglove said.

"No one definitive yet, sir. There was a report of a vagrant hooligan seen a number of weeks ago- I only just heard about it- but he's not been seen since. I've asked about and spent some time looking myself but I haven't discovered anything along that line of inquiry." Cheswick said.

"Well, we will look into it." Foxglove said and, satisfied for now with the beginnings of the investigation, pushed a dish in Cheswick's direction and pulled another toward himself. They talked far into the night.

6 THE COLOUR OF THINGS

In which Foxglove and Cheswick begin to visit each of the victims' homes, but they are waylaid by Father Leamas and his theories on the evolution of the human eye.

The next morning, Constable Caleb Cheswick was awake, but he didn't look it, hunched over a steaming cup of tea. His eyes were still rebelling against the early waking hour and his motor functions made even simple hot tea a dangerous proposition for anyone within splashing distance. He was in the Bull and Boar with a full breakfast before him but unable to comprehend it yet. Cheswick was awake and in this place against his preference because Inspector Foxglove had knocked on his door before the sun was fully up.

"How do you know where I live?" Cheswick had said, standing in his bedclothes and wondering how on earth Foxglove had found him.

"I am a detective inspector of the highest degree, Constable. The real question is; how is it you don't know how I know?" Foxglove had said.

Cheswick had stared blankly at him.

"Come, Constable, put on your clothes and join me for breakfast. We have a long day ahead of us!" Foxglove had said. He had waited in the hall for sometime while Cheswick prepared himself, splashing water on his face and stumbling about the room for his proper clothes. Cheswick had emerged at one point, fully clothed, with his slippers still on his feet. Foxglove pushed him back in, saying, "Find your boots, man!". Finally, they were seated at breakfast and Foxglove had fallen to it hardly before the plates and platters had marked the table while Cheswick looked hard at his fork, remembering his comb too late.

"Constable, please have a sip of tea. It will help. Do you always drink so much, Constable? I am concerned for you. There you are. Thank you. Now, I propose we visit the homes of the victims today and conduct our interviews. This will allow us to see the sites of the crimes and ascertain any clues which were not readily available when you were investigating." Foxglove said.

"Yes." Cheswick said. He realized saying so didn't make much sense. "I don't drink, Inspector. Not like that, anyway."

Foxglove pulled out several sheets of paper and shuffled through them. He was looking for one in particular. He read aloud as he scanned it.

"Mr Harold. Robbery. Undisclosed personal item? What was the stolen item, specifically?" Foxglove said.

"It was, erm, undisclosed." Cheswick said. He felt he still needed to defend or explain himself. "I am not used to be awakened suddenly or so loudly. I'm not complaining, you know?"

"We will need to disclose the item of Mr Harold. We cannot have undisclosed items on the official report. Why did he not disclose it, I wonder?" Foxglove said, apparently ignoring Cheswick's defense.

"He didn't say."

"That seems to be the problem. I wonder, do you have a rapport with Mr Harold? I mean, to say it indelicately; does Mr Harold trust you? What else could be his reasoning for not disclosing such important information?" Foxglove said.

Cheswick sipped his tea. He noticed the questioning eyebrow again.

"I'm sorry, Inspector. Was that a rhetorical question? I don't know that I could answer it for him." Cheswick said.

"Of course." Foxglove said.

They ate breakfast and stepped into the street. It was still just early enough for the lingering dew, shining dutifully under a sun about to obliterate it. The town was rising, too. The sounds appeared to startle Cheswick, being largely accustomed to anything this early. "I say, does that knocking go on every morning? He asked regarding the millery.

"Constable, we will be gone all day. Is there anything at home you wish to have with you today? Your notebook- is it with you?" Foxglove said.

"I am awake and fed, Inspector. I have my notebook (thank you for asking) and I am ready." Cheswick said. His enthusiasm was rising as the morning went on and he was pleased to report he was beginning to see a return to botany in his future, now that Foxglove was here and the case shortly to be wrapped up.

Foxglove looked him up and down.

"How far can you comfortably walk in those boots, Constable?" Foxglove said. It was like speaking to an unmovable wall- he would not be dissuaded from his action.

"I can walk all day." Cheswick said, still perceiving himself to be the defense.

"Hmm." The eyebrows began to ask a question, then thought better of it. "Let's be off."

They set off east from Westwich and in half an hour had reached the Blankenship estate. As they approached the gates, Foxglove spotted the rectory. The rectory stood near the road, well in front of the

Blankenship home, but on the property. It was the first building one came to when approaching the Blankenship home.

"What is that?" he asked.

"That is the rectory." Cheswick said. The Inspector's questions were beginning to unnerve him- 'how far can you walk?', 'what is that?'. Cheswick felt as though these questions had very simple answers, even obvious ones. But surely Inspector Foxglove wouldn't ask a question with such an obvious answer unless there was more to see? Perhaps Cheswick was only seeing in part while Foxglove saw in the whole?

"And Father Leamas lives there?" Foxglove said.

"Father Leamas." Cheswick said.

"Is he respected in the community, this Father Leamas?" Foxglove said.

Cheswick had never considered Father Leamas in such a light. He had always assumed Father Leamas to simply be. Nothing more.

"Of course he is respected." Cheswick said.
The eyebrows of Inspector Foxglove quivered. "Respected by all?"

Caught in an untruth, Cheswick doubled down. "Respected by all."

"Then we will drop in and get a lay of the land from the respected Father Leamas." Foxglove said, while giving Cheswick the eye. "And, even if he is not entirely respected by all, it will help us if he thinks he is."

Cheswick accepted this, silently communicating he did not fully understand it.

They stood at the door and knocked. If any man had been around to let them in, they did not acknowledge it by opening the door. There was no answer. They knocked twice more before ultimately deciding they ought to move on. It was necessary to walk back down the steps and out the smaller encasing gate before continuing on up the driveway of the Blankenships. As they performed this end around, Cheswick noticed Father Leamas in the rear garden of the house, kneeling among the shrubs.

"Oh, Inspector! There is Father Leamas!" Cheswick called.

"Where?" Foxglove said, a few steps ahead.

"Kneeling just there in bushes!" Cheswick said.

"I see him. We will not disturb him at his prayers." Foxglove said, and continued his walk.

"Pardon, Inspector. I think he is trimming the flowers." Cheswick said again, not moving from his spot. Foxglove turned around fully and screwed his eyes at the garden. A low stone wall and a small expanse of green yard separated them from the garden where Father Leamas was. Now Foxglove saw Leamas properly.

They had to shout to be heard from this distance.

"Good morning, Father Leamas!" Foxglove said. Foxglove was not a soft-spoken man but Cheswick was not prepared for the booming shout which the Inspector produced so suddenly. He jumped.

Father Leamas jumped too, from his knees, and turned around the wrong way twice before he caught sight of them. He motioned in large sweeping gestures to go back around to the front door, which they did. It was, presumably, to clean himself up a bit that took him so long to join them at the front door and welcome them into the modest dwelling. The small house with small rooms was well lit by window and lamp and nearly every flat surface was piled with small stacks of books. To make room for two guests, two stacks of books were removed from two chairs and the two men sat down while Father Leamas stood with his hands pleasantly folded.

They had already made introductions at the door and Father Leamas was clearly pleased to have Inspector Foxglove under his roof.

"My dear Inspector. I have heard of you and your dauntless struggle against crime. On behalf of Justice, let me say thank you!" Father Leamas said.

"Thank you, Father. It is my duty and my privilege to wage the war I wage. I must admit, though. There are times in the thick of the struggle I am not sure whether I am making any headway against the darkness, whether I am known or if obscurity is my destiny?" Foxglove said.

Leamas nodded his thoughts of obvious agreement. "We are called, to be sure, not to fame nor glory nor wealth. But to the truth. That is our profession, isn't it, Inspector? Our profession and, alas, our confession." He regarded Cheswick next.

"Of course, truth is found everywhere, no? A botanist sees the truth through a lens others may never, eh?"

Foxglove replied before Cheswick thought of anything proper to say. "For my part, Father, it is clear that your struggle here is a mighty one, that you are pushing back the darkness and that the people of Westwich and all the surrounding area know of your burden which you carry for them" the inspector said.

Cheswick marveled as Foxglove instantly made Father Leamas his man.

"I am grateful to have someone who sees the world as you do, under my roof, Inspector. Yes, we are doing a good work here. I am glad we are not alone." Father Leamas said. He now took another small stack of books off of a chair and sat down himself. Clearly feeling entirely at ease, he began talking about his present favorite subject.

"Are you familiar with the work being done on the evolution of the eye, Inspector?" Father Leamas said.

Whether Inspector Foxglove knew of any such work, Cheswick was sure he would never really know. He suspected Foxglove was already well acquainted with the work, however.

Father Leamas leaned into his dissertation. "Did you know, Inspector, the ancients saw only in black and white, with a little red here and there for effect? It's why all the dangerous things in nature are red, of course, to alert even our ancestors' eyes to the dangers. If danger were any other color, they would never have known." he said.

"Pardon me, but what about the green snake whose bite is so poisonous?" Cheswick said.

"I am not speaking of strict black and white; this is grayscale. Do you know what that means: grayscale? It means there are variations of the color we call gray- a scale of gray from dark to light. Or, light to dark, if that helps you understand." Father Leamas said. "I dare say the serpent in the garden was a brown snake or the woman would certainly not have been deceived. Deception, of course, is why she was deceived. No honest person is taken in by honesty!"

"This is quite fascinating, Father. Tell me, what do you know of the color of crime? We would like to hear and know your observations of the recent burglaries." Inspector Foxglove said. "In particular, we are concerned with the whereabouts of a certain man who was seen in the neighbourhood some weeks ago when the burglaries began, but who has not been seen since. We are trying to ascertain whether he might be involved in the robberies and whether he is still in the area." But he had mistimed his plea- Father Leamas had already warmed to his favorite subject and even flattery would not deter him now.

"You see, over the millennia," Father Leamas said "of which there only have been a handful since the days of creation, our eyes have developed in such a way to see the world more clearly- just as St Paul said we would see more clearly- here we are! Seeing in full color! Of course, this development occurred outside the stream called evolution which some are purporting- our eyes are not the same as the animals- but it is a parallel stream in which we swim and it is fascinating to understand."

Father Leamas went on.

"Imagine a world of black and white-" he looked pointedly at Cheswick. "Or, grayscale. Imagine a world of grayscale, and all you can see is divers shades of the one color, gray. Then, suddenly! You see something that does not fit on your scale of gray at all- you see something which, at first seems dark, dark gray- even black- but it is not quite. It is red! This vision of red is so transfixing, so fascinating and so utterly outside the realm of human experience (remember this is long ago) that it would make you, or I, or anyone stop dead in their tracks! Do you know when this first occurred? You have heard of Moses and the Burning Bush? That is no fairy tale, and no common moment- I can tell you!"

He proceeded to do exactly that.

"We know scientifically that a bush in the hot desert can spontaneously combust at any given moment. It is a disservice to the majesty and mystery of creation to attribute the burning bush episode to the mere combustion of an ordinary bush- that was a common occurrence and happens still to this day in deserts all over the world. No, gentlemen, the miracle of the Burning Bush is this; that a man saw the color of fire for the first time!"

Father Leamas' excitement rose higher.

"A bush, imbued with the presence of God, burst forth and burst through the constricting grayscale of human vision and opened a new world to the man who would lead the children of Israel out of bondage- out of slavery! Do you see the picture? The bondage of grayscale would be soon broken! The freedom of the promised land was also the promise of a new spectrum of color! Moses was called a prophet- not because he foretold freedom of slaves- God Himself had spoken that through Abram nearly four hundred years earlier! No, gentlemen, Moses was not called a prophet because he spoke. Moses was a prophet because he saw! That is why we call prophets 'seers' and not 'speachers', whatever Mr Harold tries to say to the contrary. Moses saw the true color of fire and he could by no means persuade himself it was not the Almighty Himself."

His two guests made the mistake of not preparing a diverting sentence for the brief moment of silence which followed and Cheswick simply stayed on topic with his question.

"Father Leamas, what about the rainbow which Noah saw? Or, for that matter, the green leaf which the dove brought back to him?" Cheswick said.

"I am glad you asked, my boy!" Father Leamas said. "Can you imagine being a botanist who must study dozens of gray plants- they would all look the same. You could not distinguish one from another except by the shape. What an extraordinarily dull pursuit that would be!"

"Thousands. Father. There are thousands of plants to study." Cheswick said.

"Thousands? Surely not." Father Leamas looked incredulously at the Inspector, seeking a professional assurance. "Surely not thousands. What would the Almighty need with more than, perhaps, a few hundred plants? No, the rainbow question is one which puzzled me and I am not surprised it had befuddled you. You see, the answer is this: the rainbow was in grayscale!"

"But what about the green leaf?"

"Green leaf? Who said green leaf? Does the Holy Word actually say it was green, or does it say it was an olive branch? You see, you must study and shew thyself approved- so you may answer any question a man may have. No. It was an olive leaf, after all. Of course, we know by our modern eyes that the olive leaf is green. But Noah did not see it in color. Noah saw a gray leaf and by the shape of it, knew it was an olive leaf. I wonder what they do teach you at your university! Higher learning indeed! Look at the whole of the book of Genesis and find me one instance where color was even mentioned! There is light and dark and there is grayscale."

"Surely this is only a mistake, an oversight, of the Biblical authors, to omit the mention of colour?" Foxglove said. "They must have seen just as we do. It would not occur to me, if I were performing holy writ, to point out the lack of colour. It must be taken for granted."

"No! Have you read the Iliad? The Odyssey? These works, too, contain only references to grayscale and the occasional red- signalling danger. We have indeed taken it for granted all these centuries later. Only a fool, concocting a false gospel, would have taken the pains to point out such things- the biblical authors did not point it out because they knew no different, forsooth, they saw no different, to be precise."

"Father Leamas, pardon me, but didn't Joseph receive a many colored coat from his Father, Jacob?"

"Grayscale, sir! Remember, they could see variations of the one color, gray. They, of course, just like us today- they thought they were seeing all the spectrum of color which could be seen. But we today, we are no better. Do you suppose you and I are experiencing the pinnacle, the apex of the evolution of the human eye? (He pointed at his own two eyes here) Do you suppose these see all there is to see? No, Sir! No, Sir, indeed! And recall what Esau's name was? Edom- which means red! The one color which stood for danger! That is why he could not be permitted to receive the blessing!"

"I am at a loss, Father." said Foxglove. He furrowed his brow. "If I remember my
catechism aright, the creation account includes 'every green thing', does it not?"

Leamas looked upon the Inspector kindly. "Young man." he said, (they were the same age). You do not mean to say you do not understand the Hebrew? The use of green in the creation poem is to denote new life, or, a fresh leaf. It is not meant to be descriptive in color, but in age. Our constable here, we could say he is green in his duties. That does not mean he is the color green. I think it is quite clear."

7 THE VILLAINS AT TEA

In which the Inspector and Cheswick visit with the Blankenship siblings and hear their story of the crime. Mr Blankenship introduces Foxglove to his collection of (firearms?).

It was another two hours before Foxglove and Cheswick could extricate themselves from Father Leamas' home.

"Clearly," Inspector Foxglove said. "That man is delusional."

"I wish he had answered my question about the green snake. He seemed to avoid it." said Cheswick.

"I'm sure any answer which he would have given would have been preposterous, Constable. Please advise your better self to anticipate such things and avoid those questions which lead to preposterous answers in the future." Foxglove said.

Cheswick did not reply.

The Villains at Tea

They had continued up the Blankenship driveway after their visit with Father Leamas and now stood at the residence of the siblings, ringing the bell. They did not have to wait long before being ushered in by a young girl in servant's gear. It was somehow clear they should hand her their hats and coats and they did so without being told. In Father Leamas' home, they had sat in their coats.

While it did not take long to be brought in and seated, it did take some time for Mr Blankenship to appear. They sat waiting in the drawing room.

At last a door was opened on the far end and in walked a dark man, straight and dark. How else to describe such a man? A man with his hair combed dark and his thin mustache dark, whose velvet house coat trimmed in dark and his shoes polished darker still? A man whose intentions seem dark, whose manner is dark and whose very graciousness as a host is dark? This was Mr Niles Blankenship and he was, as we have said more than once, dark.

"Oh here you are, gentleman." Mr Blankenship said darkly. "The girl told me you were in the east parlor and so I waited for you there. Stupid girl."

The two men of law had stood, waiting for their host to greet them with a handshake before sitting comfortably again. Their seats were very comfortable. While they waited for this, Mr Blankenship had a brief explanatory tirade on the domestics and their resultant culpability on all kinds of mischief in a household such as theirs.

"Inspector Foxglove." Mr Blankenship said as he shook his hand. "I am Niles Blankenship. Welcome to our home."

"Constable." Mr Blankenship said as he shook Cheswick's hand. "Please be seated, both of you."

"Thank you, Mr Blankenship. I am here to take over the burglary cases as the lead investigator."

"Thank god!" Mr Blankenship said. There was no pretense of covering his distaste for Caleb Cheswick.

"Constable Cheswick has performed his duties admirably and is now handing the case over to me. We are here today to ask you a few questions pertaining to the case, in order to clear some things up and to acquaint myself with each of the victims of the crimes. I hope that we might also speak with Miss Blankenship?" Foxglove said.

"Yes, I have asked her to join us. It would seem the domestic girl had bungled that simple request as well, since it has been several minute since I-"

Ms Blankenship appeared through a door which had opened while her brother had been speaking. As Ms Blankenship arrive in the drawing room, we pause to remind the Reader that we do not like Ms Blankenship.

Not one bit.

"I wish someone had told me you were here!" Ms Blankenship said, eyeing the young girl who had presented her at the door. "I heard voices and was forced to investigate for myself. I am glad you are visitors and not thieves or robbers!"

The two men of law stood again, bowed and sat again. They were very comfortable chairs. The Inspector repeated his introduction to her.

We are here today to ask you a few questions pertaining to the case, in order to clear some things up and to acquaint myself with each of the victims of the crimes. Thank you for seeing us."

"Of course, Inspector. Anything we can do to move this investigation out of stagnation. We are happy to assist."

"I thank you. The both of you. Now, if you will please recall for me the evening of the crime and tell me, in detail please, just what happened." Foxglove said.

"Well, Inspector, my brother and I were entertaining guests on the veranda (that's Italian for porch!). The veranda is on the back of the house, facing away from the road, so we never saw anyone approach. And as we entertained our guests, we had no idea someone was entertaining themselves in my brother's study. The idea of an uninvited guest in our home is traumatising, Inspector, I hope you can appreciate that!"

"I'm sure I cannot fathom your discomfort, Miss." Foxglove said and she clearly enjoyed being elevated in this way.

"Well, our mother- who raised us to be respectable- had left to us a large brooch of immense value and my brother kept it in a case in his study. I hope you don't think it strange that he kept it in his study- a woman's item- rather than I? Well, it is not strange at all." she said.

"I don't have to question it, as you have answered all those questions completely." Foxglove said.

Ms Blankenship (whom we do not like) resituated herself on her couch, rather than verbally replying to this, before continuing.

"Well, it was terrifying. Knowing someone had been in our house. In my brother's very inner sanctum." she was distressed but also cognizant of whether Foxglove had noted her use of Greek. He had noticed, but he also knew it was Latin.

"The strange thing, Inspector." said her brother, "was that they took only a broach. Gods know how long they were in the house, unsuspected. They did not take anything from my collection."

The Inspector took a note and did not reply.

"I say, Inspector, they did not touch my collection." Mr Blankenship said again.

"I'm sorry, Mr Blankenship, I was listening to your sister speak about the crime. Did you say collection?" Inspector Foxglove said. He did not appear interested in what the thieves did not do.

"Yes, Inspector, I have a rather sizable collection of firearms- any of which are worth fifteen times that of the broach." Mr Blankenship said. "The broach has value to us a family heirloom besides the appraised value- but the firearms are really quite valuable."

Foxglove had perked up considerably when he heard the word 'firearm'.

"I say, Mr Blankenship, are you saying you have a collection of firearms?" Foxglove said.

"Yes, Inspector. It is quite extensive- full of rare and exquisite pieces. Even some from China." Blankenship said.

"Mr Blankenship, my work as a man of law does not permit me much in the way of hobby- nor does my income allow for much in the way of collecting- but if there is one thing I have an enthusiasm for, it is firearms. The rarer, the better! You might say I am an amateur firearms enthusiast!" said Foxglove. "Would it be too forward?"

"Too forward, sir?" Mr Blankenship said. He liked to be asked.

"Might I see them, I mean?" Foxglove said.

"I should be proud to show you, Inspector." and the three men trooped off to see the collection.

Cheswick followed, bewildered. Just as he had with Father Leamas, Foxglove had established an unexpected rapport with Mr Blankenship. Was Foxglove only an expert of law, or was he also an expert of human behavior? They weaved now through a series of rooms and passages, finally entering a room lined with glass cases. A large display table lay in the center of the room, filled with what appeared to be ammunition - from several countries and, perhaps, from several time periods.

"This is really quite marvelous, Mr Blankenship! Oh, Constable, I have forgotten my hat in the other room- would you kindly obtain it for me?" said Foxglove.

"Of course, Inspector." said Cheswick.

As soon as the young man had gone, Foxglove turned to Mr Blankenship and quietly said, "Sir, please speak candidly; what is your personal opinion of Constable Cheswick?"

Mr Blankenship grew darker. "My personal opinion, Inspector, is that he is a lazy, shiftless bastard. What possible antiquated law has put him in charge is well beyond my understanding of modern civilization...-"

"No, Mr Blankenship, I meant, is he a good botanist?" said Foxglove.

"I haven't the slightest idea, Inspector." Mr Blankenship said. "Why do you ask?"

"I see." said Foxglove, replying to the answer; then he realised the question Blankenship had asked. "Why did I ask? Truthfully, I don't know. Curious."

Cheswick appeared shortly after and the conversation returned to the collection of firearms. It really was an impressive collection. Perhaps the finest for several counties. In one case were a great number of matchlock, wheellock and flintlock pistols. In another case, the same for long barrelled rifles, arranged in a similar timeline. There were a few muskets, complete with powder and balls, arranged together in one corner. Mr Blankenship had collected some few knives and swords along the way as well, but none of these were particularly good pieces. They were sued mostly to fill empty spaces between the pistols. The men focused their attention on the guns, commenting when they could from experience or from stories they had been told.

Foxglove recounted the following story.

"In Istanbul, there is a severe and secret sect of the Sikh (which the Sikh deny, of course) whose marksmanship skills are nearly unrivalled across the globe. They are, one could say, the Robin Hoods or the, well; they are expert marksmen, let us say that. Anyway, these secret sikh are hired by foreign governments to commit assassinations by long-range rifle. That is what they are skilled at, better than anyone. And they are well paid for their hellish talents.

"Perhaps you wonder why I bring this up? Well, I once hunted a man, an Englishman no less, who had been trained by this sect of the sikh in long-distance riflery. This man had murdered no less than three foreign dignitaries (and a busboy apparently by accident) during a high state dinner at no less a location than Buckingham Palace!

"You may wonder why I took the case, rather than the usual palace guard investigators? Well, the shots had been fired from outside the grounds of the palace. The man had shot clean through a window (we suppose that is how the busboy died), then proceeded to fire three distinct shots at three distincts targets through the one small hole from the first bullet. The shots were fired from the city itself- thus, although the murders took place within the palace grounds, the murder was committed outside the grounds."

"Remarkable!"

"Yes. it rather was." Foxglove said. "Three additional shots through a single hole. Even Robin Hood would have needed a little luck to win that particular competition!"

This story was not one a person could really top, it was so sensational, so the others shared stories about shooting coneys on their uncle's farm and other nonsensical tales. When they had exhausted the topic, which hadn't taken long, Foxglove said, "Might I see the place where the crime took place, Mr Blankenship? I might glean something from it."

"Of course, Inspector. Although I'm sure you will find the domestics have stupidly cleaned it since the crime. It will be sullied with their cleaning."

Again they went from room to room until they arrived at the scene of the crime: Mr Blankenship's study. Here, Foxglove appeared to leave no inch of the environment alone. He stooped to see the underside of shelves, he crawled under the desk, he tiptoed behind the drapes, he measured the room three separate times with his steps; and all the while, he asked Mr Blankenship divers questions about his habits, his schedule, his preferences.

Mr Blankenship, clearly anticipating a less intrusive inspection, was growing more annoyed by the minute and finally blurted out, "Inspector, what on earth are all these for? What possible differences can the topping on my morning toast have on the item stolen? Why, you haven't even looked at the display from where the brooch was taken!"

Inspector Foxglove stood to his full height, pausing in his inspection, and looked the man full in the face. "Mr Blankenship. In answering my questions, you have told me how much time you spend, where you spend it, and how you spend it. I am trying to understand whether you are predictable or unpredictable, vulnerable or invulnerable. I must say, though, I cannot yet determine how the thief anticipated your moods, Mr Blankenship. You are not susceptible to such crimes as these- your manners and schedule are difficult to follow. This crime is clearly the work of an expert. You have done everything I might have suggested to prevent a crime and yet, some determined mastermind has infiltrated your defenses!"

Mr Blankenship, while perhaps not understanding the method, certainly understood the compliment. "I despise a tedious life, Inspector." He said.

"Mr Blankenship, have you seen a man in town or on the moor? A stranger? This vagrant hooligan we've heard about?" Foxglove said.

"No, Inspector. Neither my sister nor I have seen such a man." Blankenship said.

"I thank you for your time, Mr Blankenship." Inspector Foxglove and Constable Cheswick took their leave and were just passing Father Leamas' garden before Inspector Foxglove made any remark.

"Mr Blankenship is the most predictable, tedious man I have ever encountered. It is a wonder his entire house was not taken while he stood in the middle of it." said Foxglove. "But I do not think I have ever sat in a more comfortable chair!"

8 REGARDING THE MOOR

In which Foxglove and Cheswick walk to the Harold house, which is some way, and talk about the landscape, and the local flavor and flora.

It was a few miles of easy walking from the Blankenship home to the Harold home. The Harolds being the next victims on the list of crimes they were now investigating together. Inspector Foxglove seemed entirely focused on the case at hand while Constable Cheswick appeared more than a little distracted by the landscape- specifically, all the new green and flowers he was seeing this week. Every leaf, petal and twig called for his attention even as Foxglove asked him questions about the case. Eventually Foxglove, realizing he would get nowhere on the present line of questioning, gave in to the distraction. He began asking Cheswick questions he thought would seem more relevant to the young man.

"Tell me about the landscape here on the north side of the, erm, moor. Com to think of it, do you call it a moor or a heath?" Foxglove said.

"We call it a moor, here." said Cheswick. "It may not be precisely correct, but our ancestors called it that and we haven't had the historic audacity to contradict it." Cheswick said.

These words were the most Foxglove had heard the young man put together into one unbroken string and so he knew he was on the right track.

"So you've kept calling it a moor? What is it like out there?" he waved a hand to his right, the south, where the moor lay.

They paused now to look over it, below the road. They saw the usual wet hills and dry hassocks. A hopelessly rocky terrain disappearing in fog even on what seemed a sunny day. Toward the center was trees and more diverse hills- quick outcroppings and sheer drops- steeper hills and dense undergrowth.

"It is land that we might have farmed once, but have established so many farms elsewhere that it is not necessary to cultivate there. Besides, that is where the Vagabonds are." Cheswick said.

"The Vagabonds? This is the first I've heard of this. What are the Vagabonds?"

"The Vagabonds are, so far as we can tell, children without family or connections. They live together as a band of outsiders. We see the results of their work much more often than we actually see them. One can stand on the edge of the moor and watch for them all day- but never notice one's picnic ha' been whisked away under your nose." Cheswick said.

Foxglove pondered this.

"Constable, I don't mean to keep harping on the subject of the crimes- but has no one implicated the Vagabonds for all these thefts? Why hasn't this come up before or entered into the report?"

"Because the Vagabonds don't break into homes, Inspector. It didn't happen."

"Constable, you are saying their gang is a gang of notorious criminals residing in the very backyard of every crime scene but there is no reason to think these criminals committed a certain crime?"

"Yes."

Foxglove thought about this too, while his eyebrows worked Cheswick over.

"I'm sorry it didn't come up, Inspector. It just isn't relevant." Cheswick said.

"Please leave it to me to decide whether something is relevant or not, Constable."

"I'd be happy to do so, Inspector. How am I to know the difference- I cannot bring up everything for your review."

Foxglove sighed.

"Let us say for now that if you are aware of any other criminals in the vicinity, that you please inform me."

"None to speak of, Inspector."

"So...- what is the makeup? I mean, the landscape of the moor?"

"This river you see? The one we are about to cross? That runs north and south- approximately. The bridge here and the bridge on the south road- near the Pimsleur's estate- are identical bridges. But if you were to follow the river from either bridge, you would come to the center of the those trees- which becomes quite a little forest in there. It is in there that the Vagabonds make their home. It is a perfect hideaway."

"Do you mean to say there is a wood in the middle of the moor? That is strange. Surely you mean a small stand of trees?"

"No."

"A thicket or brake, surely?"

"Not even that."

"A copse, perhaps?"

"No, a perfect little forest. It is quite extensive- one could get lost for some time in it."

"I am not sure we are talking about a moor or a heath now, Constable. Does it appear so to you, also? I mean, as a biologist- rather, a botanist. As a botanist, isn't the designation of moor rather off?"

"I believe it was a moor- a proper moor- at one time. Maybe the trees grew up after the moor was discovered and named so?"

"Well, I suppose that is a theory. Why wouldn't the description be updated when an entire forest (your words, I emphasise) had grown up, I wonder?"

"Tradition, I think, is the term usually applied here to excuse the citizens of the moor from keeping up to date."

"And so, the farms or estates, they all circle this moor? They all back up against, so to speak?"

"That's right."

"And are there roads or paths that cross the moor, between the various properties?"

"None that we know of. The Vagabonds seem to have some system of getting around quickly. There are a number of stories in which they've been spotted by various people in various places around the moor- seemingly at the same time though we know it isn't quite possible."

"Not possible? If they have a system of pathways, mightn't they get around rather quicker than you expect?"

"Yes. Undoubtedly. But simultaneously? No, we don't believe in magic- not even here in Westwich."

"Vagabonds. Well, I would like to speak with them. Even if they cannot have committed the crimes, perhaps they have seen something suspicious."

"I hadn't thought of that, Inspector!"

"So it would seem, Constable. Can we arrange a visit? How does one parley with them?"

"There is no going in there- no safe passage in to see them, let alone visit. I'm afraid you're out of luck on that."

"Let us give that some thought and come back to it later. For now, let us continue our walk. I think we will have to turn back for town by the time we are done with Mr and Mrs Harold."

As they continued, they came to the bridge Cheswick had mentioned as being mirrored by another bridge to the south, near the Pimsleurs. It would be unnecessary and out of place to suggest that his thoughts floated downstream- even risking the dangers of the Vagabonds- to dwell on the personage of a certain Miss Penelope Pimsleur. It is not something we will discuss here. Instead, Foxglove continued to ask for particulars about the area.

"So, how many homes or estates are situated around the moor?"

"Only a handful. Maybe seven or eight. A dozen, I think." Cheswick said.

"A handful or a dozen?" Foxglove asked.
Cheswick considered this briefly. "Yes, well. If you count the homes which are directly abutting the moor, there are only six or so. But of course, they are on the inside of the road, so to speak. Er. Imagine the moor as a carriage wheel- the road is the outer part, the estates are the spokes and the the Vagabond forest is the hub. I'm not sure that helps. I've never had to explain it before. We just speak of homes around the moor as being 'inside' or 'outside'. By

which, we mean they are directly next to the moor-inside. Or, we mean they are outside- that is, not up against the moor- those homes are outside the road. I'm sorry. This is very confusing."

"It is confusing, but I think I am following you. Do not worry. This is exactly why I am asking. I want to know the local ways- I will need to understand how the citizens of Westwich see the world of Westwich- all the ins and outs, as it were."

They walked along.

"I am envious, truth be told." Foxglove said after a while. "I like it here in the country and would likely live here if my work as a detective inspector allowed it. But, I am forced to live in the biggest cities, the noisiest places, and visit the busiest areas. It is peaceful here."

They walked along.

"I miss the bustle of the University." Cheswick countered. "Strangely enough, after living here I cannot get enough of the action of the crowds. It is odd, isn't it- that the place you grow up in can foster such things?"

"I don't think it is a fostering of one's childhood. It is a matter of balance- our souls seek balance, Mr Cheswick. We expose ourselves to one environment or another and though our soul accepts and adapts- it craves the balance it lacks. We live in one environment and think we crave another but it is the balance we crave. That is why when we have changed our environment we have only fond memories of the old."

They walked along.

"Inspector," Cheswick said. "Do you think there would have been so many varieties of plant if there had been a smaller palette of colours to begin with?"

Foxglove said nothing- which Cheswick mistook for listening, so he kept at his question.

"That is, if there were only a small selection of colors- say, a scale of only grey- from black to white. Father Leamas mentioned grayscale. I understand grayscale. Would there be such a need for so many varieties if there were fewer colors to work with? Isn't the proliferation of plants a direct result of the necessary colours at hand? What I mean to say, that is, doesn't the available selection of colours force nature's hand to make more plants? Father Leamas said Noah would have-"

At the second mention of Father Leamas, Foxglove made a rude noise.

"I know you don't think much of his theory. I don't much like it myself. I am only hypothesising. Say we had only twelve colors and the shape of a leaf to work with. How many different plants could we come up with? Not many, I think. Given that he believes what he does about the evolution of the human eye, I see how he cannot conceive of more than a few hundred plants or so." Cheswick said.

"Thank the heavens! Here is the Harold household!" Foxglove said. "Let us drop the evolution of the human eye for the moment, Constable, for now we must purge such wild theories from our minds and be prepared to engage in some intelligent conversation and- hopefully- some intelligence gathering!"

***

Constable Caleb Cheswick would have been embarrassed if Inspector Foxglove had known how often throughout that day his own thoughts had drifted toward the Pimsleur household and, in specific, Penelope. Cheswick told himself he was mentally investigating the scene of a crime- but the other four crime scenes did not have Penelope Pimsleur on premises and so those other crime scenes received considerably less attention- to whit, none. During each of their conversations that day with the victims of the crimes- the Blankenships, with the addition of Father Leamas, and later that afternoon; the Harolds- Caleb's thoughts were regularly directed toward Penelope.

When they saw Father Leamas in the garden, Caleb was imagining Penelope working in a garden. When they sat with Father Leamas in his little home, Caleb wondered whether Penelope liked to read and what books she might read. When they sat down with Mr Blankenship and his sister in their grand home, Caleb was thinking of Penelope in her own grand home. And when they men had gone into the armory, his thoughts had been on Penelope- though he did not imagine her shooting off guns. When Foxglove had asked him to retrieve his hat, Caleb was thinking of Penelope both coming and going in her own hats and what hats she might wear. And as they walked along the moor, and crossed the bridge over the river which ran north to south, Caleb's thoughts followed the quick little river down through the moor- even right past the Vagabond encampment- to Penelope and lingered there.

We can imagine that Caleb Cheswick was a reasonably intelligent young man with much capability since he was able to hold a conversation with Foxglove on the road even as he was imagining Penelope sitting in her own drawing room. But his imagination was limited because even as as he could imagine her sitting there, he could not get her to do anything other than smile- his imaginary Penelope did not sew or knit or hum to herself as she rocked in the chair. No, none of these things. She did not read or contemplate. She only sat in her imaginary chair in her imaginary drawing room (or, were they his imaginary chair and drawing room?) and smiled at him. But he was content with that.

Who is this young lady, doomed to rock in her little imaginary chair, smiling, without a care or cause? Who is this vision of domestic bliss so long as bliss is only idle domesticity? Who is this who can fill a mind from miles away? Whose white hands folded in her lap could be thus content for all eternity? This is the imaginary Penelope. She was well worth imagining and may help to explain some of the small oversights in Cheswick's investigation which would later come to light.

Penelope herself, the living breathing Penelope who exists in our world and not the imagination of Caleb Cheswick, the Penelope whom her parents would recognize was at that very moment, was thinking of Caleb Cheswick in the very manner she had since she first encountered him those several days ago on the road- that is to say; she was not thinking of him at all. Her mind was otherwise occupied and she was as untroubled by her mindlessness of him as he was troubled by his mindfulness of her.

No, Penelope Pimsleur was anticipating the dinner party her mother was putting together and she had no inclination to be occupied elsewhere. If Cheswick would have been embarrassed by Foxglove's discovery of his wandering and distracted mind, he would have been doubly embarrassed by Penelope's complete lack of bursting-hearted thoughts toward him. It would be best, for now, to not mention to him anything of the blunt reality that his thoughts are the entirety of the equation on the matter- and if it comes to it, we should let Penelope tell him herself.

Caleb Cheswick or no Caleb Cheswick, there was a party to get ready for. For the Pimsleur sisters, this meant nothing, in a functional sense, any more than any other day of the week. But less functionally, it did mean some very serious flurry regarding dresses, appearance and a general inability to focus on anything else.

It was strangely similar to Cheswick's growing fascination with Penelope. Both Cheswick and Penelope were imagining Penelope in a dress, a vision, one hand folded over the other, admired. Smiling. Always smiling. No other activity could be conjured up. Would it have changed Penelope's thoughts to know she was already admired?

Penelope's mother, Mrs Pimsleur, was however not thinking of her own self in any serene terms at the moment- she was deep in preparation and was an exacting hostess who required much of herself. For all her foibles (which do not really come into this story much) no one could have disparaged her ability as a hostess, for it was in this capacity that she truly shone forth as a singular woman. No, Mrs Pimsleur's own vision of herself was that of doing twelve things at once (usually really only two) and regardless of the task at hand was mentally engaged in so many other tasks that it might have actually been twelve.

If you were to ask Mrs Pimsleur just exactly when had she begun preparing for this particular dinner party she would tell you, after a thought, that she had never begun. Then she would correct herself and say she had always been preparing- that she could not remember a time when she had not been preparing. Assuming you produced a quizzical look as your response to her statement, she might well pick up from the kitchen table a notebook. She might open that notebook to a particular page and show you an excerpt from that notebook, where you would see notes upon notes in her looping handwriting, all of them in the manner as follows:

Mrs Danforth
  Birthday: 4/17
  Likes: Poached eggs/Boiled eggs/
  Dislikes: Raw eggs
  Delights in: Egg souffle
  Desserts: Eggless cream pie
  Reactions: Red eyes and enormous puffiness when ingesting crayfish.
  Miscellany: Usually late- invitation should include an earlier time than others so she will be on time.
***   ***

This brief excerpt would give you an excellent picture of Mrs Pimsleur as a hostess- just the kind of generous hostess who truly gives a dinner party, and doesn't simply invite people over to take compliments from them. She was, in spite of some things which we will not see in this story, a remarkable hostess. Mrs Pimsleur sat at the kitchen table, just as you would imagine, poring over this little notebook- with her invitee list beside it- refreshing her mind to each guest she had invited; their likes, their dislikes, their reactions and preferences. In this way, she would craft a dinner party in which each invited guest would feel not only welcomed, but singled out for special treatment. And it was not contrived as Mrs Pimsleur put her whole heart into the venture. As she sat, she noted one final invitation needed to be delivered- but that would have to wait for tomorrow.

All this was taking place and showing that the Pimsleur family was finding normalcy again, after the event of the robbery had shaken them. And as for Mr Pimsleur, with his daughters in their pre-party flurry and his wife in full party preparation, seized his own post-robbery normalcy by the throat and mercilessly napped. So things were coming together nicely for the Pimsleurs.

9 IN ORDER TO PAY MR HAROLD A VISIT

In which Foxglove and Cheswick arrive at the Harold home and are soon subjugated to Mr Harold's rigorous sense of grammar and despite their best efforts can make no headway in questioning him further as they struggle to utilize his impromptu vocabulary.

The Harold home sat back further from the road than any other in the neighborhood, giving it either a cozy, secluded atmosphere- or people took it as a threat to stay away. So depending on the neighbor or the mood, the Harolds' were visited or not visited mainly on this point. Foxglove and Cheswick wound their way along the drive under the chestnut trees, all gray in the shadows they created.

The Harolds- Mr Bruce and Mrs Rebecca- were part of the historic Harold family which is famous in those parts and have some of their own stories. These Harolds, Bruce and Rebecca, were on the fringe of this famous family and only really saw them at holidays or funerals. Bruce had been raised as a famous Harold and held very dearly to it and Rebecca gratefully married into the famous family- and remained grateful for her husband's tenacious claim to Harold-ness. The oddities and particulars (which every family has) of the Harold family were considered 'traits' of the famous family no matter how onerous or inconsequential. It was these types of behaviors which would get a lesser family's head slapped.

Foxglove and Cheswick were greeted at the door by Rebecca Harold and ushered into Mr Harold's library where he sat smoking. He had long white hair and a large white mustache as thick as the hair ringed around his head- as if he had merely transplanted the top of his head to his upper lip.

"We have guesters, Mr Harold." Rebecca Harold said.

Bruce Harold rose from his seat, juggling his cigar with his cane until he had a free hand to shake with both of the men.

"Gentlemen," he said and nodded to Foxglove. "Gentlemen." He said and nodded to Cheswick. "You are welcome in the Harold home."

Mr Harold meant to say this importantly and to imply that they ought to aspire to continue to be welcome in the Harold home but the two visitors thought he had suppressed a sneeze. They, in turn, introduced themselves.

"Inspector Foxglove." said Foxglove.

"Constable Cheswick." said Cheswick- the Harolds knew perfectly well who he was.

"I am at my leisure this afternoon, Gentlemen. Thus, I am at yours'. What can I do for you?" Mr Harold said. He added, "Do you smoke?"

"I would like your wife to join us, if she is also available?" Foxglove said.

The Harold's exchanged the glance of marriage and Rebecca cleared her throat and sat down in the other single chair while Bruce put out his cigar.

The two lawmen sat on the small couch and faced the Harolds.

"Thank you for your time this afternoon, the both of you." Foxglove said. "We are here, as you can guess, on the unfortunate business of the robbery perpetrated in this home some weeks ago. I am here to assume the investigation from Constable Cheswick and I would like to hear from yourselves (he nodded deferentially to Mrs Harold) just what happened the night of the robbery. Did you see or hear anything of the thief?" Foxglove said.

The Harolds again exchanged that glance that appears guilty but only means they are waiting for the other to speak. "No. We did not." said Mrs Harold.

"I did not hear or see anything myself." said Mr Harold. "But pardon me, Inspector. How do you know it was a thief?"

"A theft always requires a thief, of course." Foxglove said. But one could see he answered the question before pondering it and now his eyebrows were working the matter through. "What do you mean, Mr Harold? Surely you do not mean something was not stolen? Do you mean someone within the household may have taken it? I read the report- I did not think the butler... but, I get ahead of myself. Please, what do you mean by the question?" Foxglove said.

"I mean, Inspector, just this; how do you know it was a thief? Was there any evidence of a thief, exactly?" said Mr Harold.

"Mr Harold. Was something stolen or not?" Foxglove said.

"There was." said Mr Harold.

"So, something was stolen- therefore a theft occurred. A theft requires a thief. It is only grammatical sense." Foxglove said.

"Ah-ha! That is the question, Inspector! It is a question of grammar- you are right there. Let us examine." Mr Bruce Harold said.

Mrs Rebecca Harold sat quietly, upright in her chair, hands folded pleasantly in her lap. She was a Harold, after all. Mr Harold continued.

"Inspector, I am surprised. You have a greater reputation than this. You have, without evidence, identified a thief-" said Mr Harold.

"I have not identified a thief- I have only said there was a thief." Foxglove said.

"But you have identified a thief. You have identified the theft as having been perpetrated by a man!" said Mr Harold.

"Most thieves I come across are men." But once again, Foxglove answered the question too quickly. "Mr Harold. What do you mean?"

"Inspector, you said the crime was committed by a thief. Is that correct?" said Mr Harold.

"Yes. I hope so." Foxglove said.

"That is a claim for which you have no evidence. There is not evidence there was a thief any more than there is no evidence for the theft having been committed by an elephant!" said Mr Harold.

"But we do agree there was a theft, Mr Harold?" Foxglove said.

"Of course, Inspector. The evidence is all there. There was indeed a theft." said Mr Harold.

"Does that not necessitate a thief? By definition, I mean?" Foxglove said.

"Of course not. A theft simply means we have a thief, a thiefess or thieves." said Mr Harold.

"I understand thieves, Mr Harold. You are right, there may have been more than one thief." Foxglove said.

"That is certainly not what I am saying- so I am certainly not right about it. Although I admit it may be true." said Mr Harold.

"Mr Harold." Foxglove said, not knowing how to continue.

"Mr Harold," said Rebecca. "Perhaps the Inspector would benefit from a grammatical understanding of his error. It appears he is in ignorance of the situation."

"Ah, of course, my dearess, thank you." said Bruce. He turned back to Inspector Foxglove. "The question, Inspector, is not a question of whether there has been a theft- you have made quite clear there has been a theft. Your error is in assuming, without evidence, that it was perpetrated by a thief- a man."

"Mr Harold?" Foxglove said.

"You are operating under a delusion of the English language. You assume that a theft necessitates a thief. That is not the case. A theft can be committed- in fact, any crime can be committed by either a man or woman." said Mr Harold.

"That is true." Foxglove said.

"Therefore! A crime can be committed by a thief or a thiefess. A man or a woman." said Mr Harold.

"Mr Harold, excuse me, I don't think there is such a word as 'thiefess'." Foxglove said.

"And that, Inspector, is the delusion of the English language under which you are laboring. It has limited your investigation already!" Mr Harold adjusted himself in the chair as he undertook the lesson. "Imagine the freedom and insight available to us beyond language, Inspector! The English language restricts us- we must break free if our generations are to be free." said Mr Harold.

In Order to Pay Mr Harold a Visit

"Mr Harold, when I say 'thief', I mean either a man or woman." Foxglove said.

"But that is the difficulty, Inspector. You mean- but you do not say. The language you are utilising binds your hands, as it were. Let me explain, and perhaps I can open your mind to a more open investigation. Consider this; that if one is to be an admirer, one must have an admiree. Now, you will say admiree is not necessarily a proper word, but you get the idea. That is, it strikes me that we do not have a more direct linguistic connexion between the two persons in the case of admiration. Further, it would be helpful in quiet conversation and hushed tones to easily distinguish persons by such method- to whit, I propose the following terms which I expect will be helpful in providing clarity and avoiding unnecessary gossips; the admiress (a woman) an admirer (a man) an admiree (a man also- but to whom the admiration is directed) and finally the admiree-ess (of course, a woman to whom admiration is directed). There, I think that about covers it for admiration.

"But let us consider the present scenario. Theft. We therefore must speak plainly and clearly. So, if a theft has occurred, then we have either a thief (a man who has committed a theft) or a thiefess (a woman who has committed a theft). (Or, of course, some combination of those) On the other hand, we must consider the victim- but victim is an unfortunate word we must do away with. So, we must apply simple reasoning to the situation and say a victim of a theft is better understood as either a 'thefter' (a man against whom a theft has been committed) or a theftess (a woman against whom a theft has been committed). This is a much more satisfying grammatical solution to the problem.

"So, in the present situation of the theft committed here at the Harold household, you have in residence both a thefter (myself) and a theftess (my dear Rebecca). What you categorically do not have is evidence of a thief- although it may come to light there was in fact a thief. Do you understand your situation better now, Inspector?"

Foxglove said nothing and there was something of a brief silence, lasting only a moment.

"So, will you be investigating the robberies while you are here, Mr Foxglove?" Rebecca Harold said. She was a Harold, after all.

Inspector Foxglove rose. Cheswick followed his lead.

"Mr Harold. Mrs Harold." Foxglove said. "It is time for us to go."

Inspector Foxglove had made a brief and forcible exit from the Harold household, verbally dragging Cheswick (who barely caught hold of his own hat on the way) out the door with him. The Harolds were unable to get a word in edgewise as Foxglove had kept up a barrage of Pardons, So-Sorrys, Official Business, Must-Hurrys and Good-days all the way from the sitting room couch to the front door and beyond. It was as if a siren had gone off in his head, and he let the Harolds think his superior detective skills had been alerted to a crime in progress in some other region. Foxglove and Cheswick were halfway down the drive when Cheswick remembered to say goodbye to the Harolds but all he could do was turn and wave ineffectively at the now-closed front door.

"Constable, we must assess our stratagem. Your victims are the most impossible collection of nitwits and imbeciles I have ever encountered in a single town- and I realize with great trepidation that we have interviewed hardly half of them yet. The remotest possibility of extracting any information whatsoever from these people will hinge entirely on our ability to extract and will in no way reflect their ability to produce it. We must overcome this buffoonery somehow."

Here, Foxglove stopped dead in his tracks and, squaring his shoulders to Cheswick, offered his hand and shook the other's hand firmly. "I commend you, noble Constable, in your herculean efforts and stunningly effective results in producing the interviews and information which you already have. I admit to underestimating your skill and prowess. When I first laid eyes on your report- at the District, of course- I freely admit my disappointment and concerns regarding your worthiness as a constable and officer of the law.

"But now. But now, sir! Having spent a brief hour combined with your townspeople, I am stunned you got as much information as you did, that you were as thorough as you were and, if I may say as one of the foremost champions of justice in our fair land- your reports were excellent and beyond thorough."

Foxglove shook Cheswick's hand again after this but did not give him a moment to respond- he immediately turned them back to the road back to Westwich proper.

"We must devise a strategy and it must be, I see now, tailored to each interview. A bespoke interrogation, if you will. You must inform me, to the greatest degree of detail, what you know of each of the victims beforehand so that I am not blindsided like a ship's captain in the fog."

"I think I could do that." Cheswick said.

"I am hesitant about this, truth be told. I like to let the facts speak to me without preconceived ideas given to me by third parties (with all due respect to yourself, Constable). But in this particular case, it is clear we must take this tack. Good. Now, for starters, what on this good brown earth was that Mr Harold babbling about?" Foxglove said.

"Mr Harold is obsessed with grammar, which you have deduced. He has a litany of rules for our common language which only he can fathom- his wife, of course, is only too happy to be a Harold (famous or not) and acquiesces to any and all linguistic demands he makes. What you witnessed is the result of sobriety, so to speak." Cheswick said.

"Are you saying we must endeavor to get him drunk before he will talk sense?!" Foxglove said.

"No. Only that it helps tremendously if one has imbibed before talking too seriously with him. It merely helps." Cheswick said.

They walked on while Foxglove pondered this.

"I am not sure that is a strategy, Constable. But at least we are talking about taking steps." Foxglove said. "Now, what about this Mr Rampert? And what is Huffington-in-Box?"

"Mr Rampert suffers from a condition of coughing. It renders him nearly incapable of completing a sentence. I'm not sure anyone in the neighborhood has ever had an entire, comprehensible conversation with him." Cheswick said.

"That is a strange malady. I have heard of that before- but in that other case, it was because the man did not want to have a conversation in the first palace and pretended to cough horribly." Foxglove said.

"And no one questioned it?" Cheswick said.

"Have you ever questioned it of Mr Rampert? Besides, it is difficult to question someone who keeps interrupting your most important question. Mr Rampert will certainly be a challenge. So then, what is this Huffington-in-Box?" Foxglove said.

"The name of the estate. Years ago, Lord Huffington- to whom Mr Rampert is not at all related- came under significant financial duress and was forced to sell the estate to cover his losses. Probably gambling losses or, some said, he kept a woman in London who robbed him blind. Anyway, it was Mr Rampert who had the perfectly timed inheritance of liquidated monies and was able to purchase the estate in its entirety- both sides of the road- for himself. To my knowledge he, like Lord Huffington, has no child or heir. He is quite getting on in years and I have heard some question in town regarding the future of the estate. So, the estate is in question. There is some speculation it will revert to the previous owner but no has seen or heard from Lord Huffington in some years." Cheswick said.

"You said the estate spans the road?" Foxglove said.

"Yes, there is extensive property on both sides on the east road. In fact, there is an abandoned cottage in the far reaches which no one has used in years. As a child, I imagined it to be a den of robbers." Cheswick said.

Foxglove smiled. "That may well be. Do you think now, as an adult, that is where your Lord Huffington might be hiding?"

"Inspector! That is stunning! I'd never thought if it... Though now you say it, I can recall young Penelope Pimsleur speculating just such an idea when we were very young. I called her too young and childish- myself only a child." Cheswick said.

"Pimsleur, eh? Isn't that the surname of one of our victims? Was it the same, meaning, she who was robbed, then?" Foxglove said.

"No. Well, yes. But no. It was her father, Mr Pimsleur, who had some items stolen. She still lives there. The whole family does."

"Yes, Constable. They often do." Foxglove said.

"On the other hand, returning to the estate, if it does not return to the previous owner- provided he is not found to be lurking there already!- then there is serious question whether the estate will be abandoned and whether the citizens ought to step in and do something." Cheswick said.

"Such as?" Foxglove said.

"I've not heard any specifics on that. Only the speculation. The actual something which the citizens ought to do is left very vague." Cheswick said.

"Inactionable. Nothing will come of it. I recommend you, as Constable, take a swift approach on the topic and make a plan so you do not have an entire estate languishing, waiting for your childhood robbers to make a den of it. Where is Onegin when you need him, eh?" Foxglove said.

"Pardon, Inspector? Onegin?" Cheswick said.

"Russian. It is only a story, Constable. I thought you might know the reference from University?" Foxglove said.

"Ah, perhaps. But not that I distinctly recall." Cheswick said. "But, back to the Pimsleur family- the one in which Penelope lives, or is a part of and lives with her family- they are a highly respectable family and well-off. Not that Penelope acts haughtily, as though they are well-off, which they are. She is very demure."

Foxglove waited, expecting Cheswick to continue but the young constable was already patrolling an imaginative room where the Miss Pimsleur sat in her rocking chair (or was it his rocking chair?) with her hands folded (demurely) in her lap.

"And what else of the Pimsleur family, Constable?" Foxglove said.

"Oh, they are very well-respected and, well. Hm. They are normal. I think that may be the best way to say it." Cheswick said.

"Normal? What do you mean by normal?" Foxglove said.

"I mean they are more like those in town than those on the moor. The moor is almost a different world than town. It is a strange divide between the two populations. The Williams, for instance, live in town and when you meet them it will be as if you are talking with someone quite normal. Of course, I understood none of this until I went away to university. I don't know whether anyone here actually recognises the disparity." Cheswick said.

"Yes, but what do you mean by normal?" Foxglove said.

"By normal, I suppose I mean that there are no strange eccentricities, no bad manners, no mysterious fortunes or bizarre rules about grammar. They have no foibles to speak of. They are not the subject of gossip. They are well-liked, well-respected and their parties are well-attended. They will, the whole family, greet you the same in the lane or in their own home. There do not seem to be any secrets among them nor secrets which they hold back from the outside world- I know that is the idea of a secret, but one can often tell when an entire family is holding back a dark secret." Cheswick said.

"Can one?" Foxglove said.

"Oh yes. Perhaps you read mysteries, like I used to, which are full of furtive glances and clearing throats and veiled threats and excuses like 'family business' and shouting in the next room but when they come into the room they are all smiles and friendly greetings?" Cheswick said.

"That does not sound like the sort of books I read. In fact, those do not even sound like proper mysteries at all. In that case, it would be clear from those furtive glances and veiled threats and overt clues that something is most certainly amiss- no mystery there. No, Constable, I would argue that a proper mystery is one in which everything appears, as they say, tip-top- and only a real detective can cipher out that a mystery exists at all. Any policeman can strike a target if it is given to him. But it takes a true, keen detective inspector to strike a target which no one else can see." Foxglove said.

"A target which no one else can see, Inspector? Is that possible?" Cheswick said.

"It is, my boy. Listen, I was in London one day and noticed three separate and seemingly unrelated occurrences- none of which caught my eye or attention of their own merit- but the combination of them set my keen detective sense ablaze. One was a newspaper advertisement while sitting in a boarding house having breakfast. The second was a remark I overheard about the coming weather while having my hat resized and cleaned. The third was an observation I made on a railway station platform which decorum will not permit me to recall for you.

"These are all to be noticed and cast away in an instant- but together, they are so much more than the sum of their parts! I knew, while still in the haberdashery, something was afoot and the interaction on the train platform merely confirmed it. Was I the only policeman in London to read the newspaper, notice the weather or to stand on a train station platform that day? Of course not! But that is what separates me from the ordinary policeman.

"What separates me from the ordinary policeman is my ability- both natural to me and well-developed over the years by trial and difficulty and determination- to hold loosely to each piece of information, each observation, each conversation, each detail in the atmosphere, landscape and tribulation around me. To hold them loosely, each of them, and allow them to sift and sort in my hand (so to speak) and distill from them the important from the important, the chaff from the wheat and to examine those fine kernels. Those kernels, so carefully curated by my intellect, are the necessary clues to solving a crime." Foxglove said. "That is what I was doing that day at breakfast, at the haberdashery and finally on the train platform. Winnowing and distilling. Finding clues which everyone has access to, but neither the patience or wit to see it."

"What happened that day, Inspector?" Cheswick said.

"A notorious and particularly devious criminal named Orton Black was planning a heist that would shake Scotland Yard and the whole of Londinium." Foxglove said.

When he had said the name, Orton Black, a new and strange look entered Foxglove's eyes. Cheswick observed the change but was uncertain of how to interpret it.

"So, you foiled the heist? You caught this Orton Black?" Cheswick said.

"No. I did not foil him. Nor did I catch him. He has eluded me for years, truth be told. He has eluded all of us men of law." Foxglove said. "But I have nearly caught him- been within mere steps of him but he has always managed to escape at the last minute. No one else can say they have been so close to catching him as I. But it is not enough! I must be the one to catch him." Foxglove said.

"He is quite notorious, then?" Cheswick said.

"Infamous! And my great and selfish fear is that some knuckle-dragging policeman on beat will accidentally apprehend him for loitering and earn the prestige for which I am due. I have chased this Orton Black too far and too long-"

Foxglove now turned to Cheswick a steely eye which would have frightened the young man in another scenario where justice were not so precious at stake.

"I consider Orton Black to be my sole and lawful prey." Foxglove said.

10 MR RAMPERT IS MIRACULOUSLY CURED

In which Mr Rampert is miraculously, albeit briefly, cured for a few minutes of conversation.

Foxglove and Cheswick, and now referred to as such in the community, had taken an early dinner and went their separate ways that night, with the intention of meeting up again the next morning for breakfast and the formation of a plan for speaking with Mr Rampert (he of the immutable cough).Foxglove had already decided he might visit the Pimsleurs on his own for fear Cheswick might ask ridiculous questions about Penelope's whereabouts at the moment and start sketching her in his little botany notebook. Cheswick's growing fascination with the young Miss Pimsleur was not a bother to Foxglove, but considered it might well be a hindrance to the investigation so he sought to mitigate the effect of Cheswick's involvement.

With this aim in mind, Foxglove liveried a phaeton and sped down the West Road to the south of the so-called moor, then turned onto the South Road and drove to the Pimsleur estate, which impressed him very much. This additional visit after a day of exhausting visits tells us at least one thing about this man, that is; regardless of what else might be said later of him, he was certainly energetic in his focus on the investigation. But, and perhaps to Constable Cheswick's credit, Foxglove's interview with Mr Pimsleur uncovered no new information regarding the burglary. Foxglove was not the sort of man to be put off by this or consider it a wasted trip- instead, he left the estate confident all that could be known for now was known.

So, at breakfast that next morning, Foxglove broached the subject of Cheswick's affections and the possible impact on the investigation at hand.

"Mr Cheswick, it is important for me to raise a topic of conversation which I hope will be constructive and beneficial to us both." Foxglove said. "The topic is sensitive, but the nature of it requires me to raise it expeditiously. I will get right to the point. It is this: your affections for Miss Pimsleur are on the cusp of interfering with our detective work."

Cheswick opened his mouth to protest but Foxglove stopped him with a raised hand.

Mr Rampert is Miraculously Cured

"You affections are clear, sir, but I am not here to squelch them. I am here to speak of them honestly and plainly so that we may bring them out into the open where they can do no harm. Yes, harm. If we are to continue this investigation together, it must be in a unified and direct assault until we learn the truth behind the robberies. We cannot have both an investigation and a courtship happening simultaneously, the fact of which I hope you can comprehend." Foxglove said.

Cheswick sat flabbergasted. He had been certain his thoughts of Penelope were well hidden and he now felt himself in the presence of a real detective.

"Inspector, I must-" Cheswick said. Or rather, began to say but Foxglove interrupted him.

"Mr Cheswick, if you are about to deny the affections which you not only hold closely but broadcast loudly, let me stop you. You are in love with Miss Penelope Pimsleur. Let us assume no more needs to be said to confirm that. Let us move on now to the timing of this matter. You must, I pray you, withhold your declarations of love until the proper time." Foxglove said.

"Then I won't deny what is so obvious to you, Inspector." Cheswick said.

"Well, that is a start, Mr Cheswick. For now, please withhold your intentions until we have identified our burglar. I suspect we are perilously close to a positive identification but we have to be certain. Beyond any doubt. Do you understand?" Foxglove said.

"I understand, I think. I am to wait to speak to Miss Penelope until we have identified the burglar. Is that correct?" Cheswick said.

"Yes, that is exactly correct." Foxglove said.

"But, Inspector, how does this have any bearing on the investigation? Identification or otherwise?" Cheswick said.

"Because, Constable, I have let it be known in some quiet circles that I suspect these crimes to be what is called in those circles, 'an inside job'. It is important, in those circles, that this be believed to be true." Foxglove said.

"As much as I desire to understand what you are saying, I am afraid I don't." Cheswick said.

Foxglove's eyebrows weighed the veracity of this claim.

"Well, that would be a good sign, if you did not understand. What it means is that the criminal underworld, as we speak, is under the impression that the great Inspector Foxglove suspects these robberies have been committed by one of the residents who claims to have been robbed. That is what an inside job is- someone quite literally on the inside of the house has committed the crime." Foxglove said.

"Astounding! How did you figure this out with such scant evidence? And does this mean we have five criminals to catch, and not just one? I assumed it was all the work of the same criminal!" Cheswick said.

"It is the same criminal in each and every case, Constable. And, to be quite clear, it is not an inside job. As I said, I have led others to believe that I believe it is an inside job. I pretended to let it slip quite by accident- on purpose, I assure you. Now, the real criminal, when he hears of this, will let his guard down ever so slightly. I propose it will be just the window we need to identify him and bring him in." Foxglove said. "However, if you go getting engaged to one of the implied suspects, it will let the true criminal know something is up."

All this was spoken so calmly, so confidently, so masterfully by Foxglove that Cheswick again marveled. Foxglove continued.

"Now then. Regarding Miss Pimsleur. I believe we will have identified our thief in a few short days and after, you will be entirely free to speak to her. In any other situation, I would have no reason and no leverage to prevent you but in this case, this criminal case, I must implore you to wait. Will you wait just a few short days, Mr Cheswick?" Foxglove said.

"Of course, Inspector. I will wait until you allow it." Cheswick said.

"It is agreed then. That is good. Now, we have an appointment with Mr Rempert this afternoon; so let us be going." Foxglove said.

Once again, Foxglove and Cheswick set out walking to make a visit on the moor. The day was bright already- as every spring day seems brighter and earlier as the weather warms- and the mud was in full force. They arrived at Mr Rampert's home and were escorted in promptly and while the visit began as Cheswick anticipated, it did not continue that way. Mr R received the men with the same coughing and complaining and coughed on the bureau looking for his handkerchief and after a brief interval of calm in which Foxglove formally introduced himself, coughed again. Mr Rampert, when asked, began telling them the story of the burglary which had occurred at his home only a few weeks earlier.

"I was kkhaaw in the gar- kkhaawwl garden all hhhwwkk hhhwwwkk khaaaaaak day." He said. "I was in ghaaak in the garden. Hck hck. I was in the garden."

And so Cheswick thought it would continue. But Foxglove had other ideas.

"Mr Rampert. Allow me to ease your condition while I tell you a story." Foxglove said.

"HCcck. By all means, INspec- Hcchk! Inspec- Hhuhk!, sir." Mr Rampert said.

"In my experience as a detective inspector, i have come across all manner of scoundrels and villains. I recall once, when in the great city of Birmingham, I was delayed in my investigation by an individual who had much the same condition as yourself. Truly! Although I had a list of suspects, I could never quite get all the information I needed from this one key witness- or rather, I believed him to be a key witness until I noticed him from a distance one day in a cafe,

Mr Rampert is Miraculously Cured

holding forth in normal conversation with nary a sneeze, let alone a hack or cough. When I saw him again, I confronted him and, by careful examination, both called his bluff and arrested him on the spot. He, of course, was the real culprit in that crime and had he not drawn so much attention to himself by his pretended malady, I may never have caught him."

Mr Rampert gazed silently, appearing to stifle the slightest cough.

"Now, Mr Rampert, let me assure you; I am not investigating anything other than a simple robbery. If there is any malfeasance regarding real estate law, or inherited property or missing persons, it well outside the purview of my present investigation." Foxglove raised a finger. "However, if I am hindered in my present investigation, I may see fit to open another. Do we understand each other, Mr Rampert?"

Mr Rampert adjusted himself in his seat once or twice and mildly cleared his throat and spoke.

"Yes, Inspector, I believe we do. So let me say, simply, that the silver which was taken was valuable, but not nearly so valuable as other things which I keep in the house, or elsewhere. Certainly, if I were being purposely targeted, I imagine those valuables would have been taken and the silver left behind." Mr Rampert said.

"I see, Mr Rampert. And are these other valuable articles ones that could be carried off just as easily as the silver was?" Foxglove said.

"Oh yes, just as easily. Clearly, the thief had no idea what was actually available to him. I have heirlooms worth a thousand silver spoons in my bedroom safe. Jewels, ancient coins, and the like." Mr Rampert said.

"Clearly, the thief did not plan properly- if I may say so." Foxglove said. "The silver which was stolen, is it in any close proximity to the heirlooms you've described?"

"No. Not at all. The bedroom where the safe if kept is on the third floor at the far end of the house, while the kitchen lies here on the first, at the very opposite end. It was only convenience which kept the thief from combing the house." Mr Rampert said.

"Yes, I daresay. Hmm. This is very enlightening, Mr Rampert. I have no further questions. You have been most helpful." Foxglove said.

"I am glad to have been of service?" Mr Rampert said.

"Yes, most certainly. I will not trouble you further." Foxglove said.

Mr Rampert coughed just a little.

"Well, Constable, shall we be going?" Foxglove said.

Since leaving Mr Rampert at Huffington-In-Box, the pair had walked in silence. More than once, Cheswick had thought to ask about Mr Rampert and what he had witnessed in the miraculous, though momentary, recovery. As he closed the door behind them, Mr Rampert had begun in again with a violent

Mr Rampert is Miraculously Cured

coughing fit as he bid them 'good-day'. Foxglove's story about a criminal who pretended to cough seemed both absurd and wonderful. What possible reason would the owner of Huffington-In-Box have for not wanting to be questioned? What secret could that wall of annoyance be hiding? Did it have anything to do with the case at hand?

"I have a growing suspicion, Constable." Inspector Foxglove said and then was silent.

Cheswick pondered this and decided he did not yet have enough information to ask an intelligent question. He was formulating a simple request for more information when the Inspector spoke again.

"It has been growing in a small corner of my mind, for some days now." Foxglove said.

"What is it regarding?" Cheswick said. He was grateful the question he had been forming was still relevant.

"Regarding, Constable? It is regarding this case, I can assure you." Foxglove said. "Yes, it has been growing in my mind since the day we spoke to that cleric."

"Father Leamas? Is he a cleric? I thought he was a rector?" Cheswick said. He meant this as a corrective statement, disguised as a question, allowing the Inspector to make the correction himself.

"Cleric. Priest. Parson. It is all the same. I prefer rabbi, myself; I believe it has a stronger working." Foxglove said.

"A rabbi? Isn't that a term the Jews use for something? A parson, I think. A Jewish parson." Cheswick said.

"The word means Teacher. The Book says it plainly enough, Constable. But I do believe we should say 'rabbi' rather than 'parson'. I think it is too strong a word- the idea that one man can shepherd a group of men is too much. Can one man teach another? Of course. But to guide him? Provide him spiritual direction? Not likely. But, we get off the subject." Foxglove said. "The suspicion which has been growing quietly in my mind has manifested itself in light of this latest conversation. Do you remember the story I told you? The story of how I nearly caught the notorious Orton Black? In it, I told you I had a number of seemingly disconnected coincidences which, in sum, pointed me to the criminal." Foxglove said.

"Yes, Inspector, I remember that." Cheswick said.

"That strange and nagging suspicion which I now have is strangely similar to that day. I believe my subconscious has picked up on a trail, miniscule and obscure- but I believe we are onto something very important. In this case." Foxglove said.

"What is it?" Cheswick said.

"It is not that we have new information, necessarily, but that we have confirmed something rather unexpected." Foxglove finally said.

"I am at a loss, Inspector. What have we confirmed?" Cheswick said.

"Let me begin with a few facts. First, were any of the robberies in this case of any significance in and of themselves?" Foxglove said.

"Well, no. They were, each of them, quite small. A puzzle to the last, but the value- if that is what you are referring to- was not monetarily significant." Cheswick said.

"Right. Second, in each of the cases, were there not in fact, actual items of significant value in each house?" Foxglove said.

"Yes. Yes, Inspector, that is true." Cheswick said.

Foxglove nodded significantly.

"What does that mean, Inspector? What is the suspicion?" Cheswick said.

"Constable, let us say you are the thief- No! Je n'accuse pas! You are quite innocent, of course. I merely mean, that if we look at this case from the perspective of a thief, we may gain some insight. You remember I told you that in order to catch the thief, one must think like a thief? Well, if a thief were to steal something, what would be the purpose of stealing something of lesser value when something of greater value is available in the very same house? What kind of thief would do so?" Foxglove said.

"I hadn't thought of it that way. I suppose if I were a thief, which I am hesitant to even mention, I would certainly want to make the most of my risk in breaking into another man's home. It is a dangerous gamble in the first place, so it would make sense to leave with value commensurate with the crime." Cheswick said. He reflected. "That is a discomfiting thought."

"It is a delicate technique, is it not? To put yourself in the place and mind of a criminal? But that is the darkness we tread as champions of the law, Constable. It is necessary we go to that place so others do not." Foxglove said.

"But what does it all mean in this case? Or, in these cases?" Cheswick said.

"It means that not only are all these cases connected, it means they are connected in more ways than one- I may be saying too much when I say there may be a sinister connection we do not yet fathom." Foxglove said.

"Sinister? What do you mean, Inspector?" Cheswick said.

"I cannot yet say, Constable. Not for secrecy- but because I do not know." Foxglove said. "But, in all but one case, items of lesser value were stolen when items of greater value were available. But each of the crimes has a similar value- including that of the Williams. None of the crimes were enough to cause you to summon the district, but taken together, you were forced by protocol to contact the district. We have, on one hand, a thief who does not take enough- but who, on the other hand, takes just enough to involve more policeman. The first speaks to a simple thief, the second speaks to an idiot. The first speaks to a mere crime wave which is likely already over- the second speaks to a larger plan we have yet to apprehend. That means the first instance is a petty thief- one we can catch easily enough and who is likely in another town already, starting his cycle over. But that means the second speaks to an idiot with a plan. The second is very much worse." Foxglove said.

Cheswick was trying to follow all this. "Could an idiot thief perpetrate so many crimes successfully? That does not speak to an idiot, does it?" Cheswick said.

"No, it does not, Constable. That may well be the growing suspicion- that we are not dealing with a petty thief, nor an idiot thief. Let us say, for the moment, that it is neither and that we are in fact dealing with a thief of some considerable skill who also has a plan we do not yet perceive." Foxglove said.

"What kind of plan could that thief have? He has already stolen several items of value- all told, he could pawn all of it for a tidy sum. If he moves on to another town or village, as you say, then that is the plan, is it not? To move on before he can be apprehended?" Cheswick said.

"We must ascertain the goal of our thief. There are two immediate possibilities which come to mind, Constable. One, the goal may be to steal just enough to get away and make his living that way. But Two, the goal may be the very game of it all. This thief- if he is both skilled and cunning- may perceive all this as a game." Foxglove said.

"And ruin people's lives? To put them at such dis-ease and on their guard? To invade the privacy of private citizens all for the sake of a game? Who would do such a thing? What kind of person, let alone a thief, would act out a game which harms so many?" Cheswick said. He was quite put off and incensed by the idea.

"A monster, Constable. We rightly refer to such a man as a monster. It is a monstrous act, perpetrated by a monster. And it is exactly the kind of thing a devious man like Orton Black would do." Foxglove said.

"Orton Black? The notorious criminal you told me about? What could possibly draw such a man to a small village like Westwich?" Cheswick said. He felt the weight of these evil possibilities on his shoulders now.

Foxglove pondered the constable's rhetorical question a moment. "Orton Black and I are rivals. It is entirely possible that he has kept tabs on me and knows my whereabouts- I do not hide like a common criminal, I move about as a free and honest citizen- and in knowing my whereabouts, has planned all this so as to draw me here to Westwich. Yes! That would explain why the crimes totaled such a value as to force you to contact the district when you did- he, knowing I was assisting with the operations there."

Foxglove said. "He is attempting to draw me into one of his games!"

Foxglove and Cheswick had come to the doorway of the tavern.

"I believe these crimes are my fault, Constable. I have failed to bring Orton Black to justice and now he has brought violence to your village- only to mock me." Foxglove said. Leaving Cheswick standing before the tavern door, Inspector Foxglove spun on his heeled boot and, in impossibly long strides, walked out of town in the direction of the moor. A cyclone could not have been a more imposing threat than the famous Inspector Foxglove in his fury.

11 THE DINNER PARTY

In Which Mrs Pimsleur Hosts What Turns out To Be One of Her Most Exciting Dinner Parties "Someday the parties of this neighbourhood may be hosted in drab colors, with paper plates and wilted lettuce! But today is not that day! Today is Elegant!"

No one had seen or heard from Inspector Foxglove in three days. But he was the talk of the party that night at the Pimsleur residence. All the planning of Mrs Pimsleur had come together at just the right time and everything was set and prepared for her loveliest dinner party to date. Each guest was invited and anticipated according to their likes and dislikes, their interests and patterns.

Precisely at six that evening, then, Mrs Pimsleur was positioned at her place in the drawing room with pre-dinner tastings. Pre-dinner tastings because she disliked the french words of *aperitif* or *hors d'oeuvres*, and disapproved of the italian *appetizer*, ("Why can't they just say what they mean?" she would ask) and the truth is, had she known the spanish *tapas*, she would have found a way to reject that as well. Mrs Pimsleur was a very disciplined woman that way. The guests arrived by twos and threes in an order which does not really concern us, but the first to arrive was Mr Blankenship and his sister. A housemaid let them in and took their outer things from them gently, as she did with each guest.

The evening followed the standard protocol of a Pimsleur gathering, which meant pre-dinner in the drawing room (where hardly anyone drew anything, followed by dinner in the dining room (where everyone dined) and desserts were served on the veranda (this italian word was meant with no hostility) on one of the first nights of that spring on which it was just warm enough to be outdoors after sunset. The guests, some of whom we have met, and others we have not, filled the rooms over and over so one could hardly get about expect to dance.

Mr Bruce Harold and his wife, Mrs Rebecca Harold presumed to hold court in the drawing room, placing themselves nearest the fireplace and standing as if to preside from there over the entire gathering. They occasionally would lean, one to the other, and making a grave, quiet comment to which the other would solemnly nod. The other guests came and paid their respects but left them generally just as quickly.

Mr Rampert coughed and hacked an atmosphere about his person which made approaching him difficult and kept the other guests in a perfect orbit around him like germ-free satellites. Anyone who attempted close proximity maneuvers or attempted direct contact were regaled with the story of the burglary in his home, staccatoed with more coughing than even a sick person can produce.

A close observer of Mr Blankenship would have witnessed another orbital stratagem at work. His movements, in the sitting room, his eyes at dinner, and his actions on the veranda were in regular rotation all around a celestial object, being gravitationally pulled as he was. But no one noticed this, least of all the celestial object.

Ms Blankenship, the sister, (whom we dislike to a nearly unreasonable degree) was merely (to our own view) a black hole putting on the airs of a charming nebula. That is all we hope to say about her.

Father Leamas kept moving from one conversation to another the entire night. He never seemed to be in a conversation or diversion of his own, but always attached to that of another. In each instance, having assumed a position, would comment on the bright colors of the room, or the settings, or the fruit, or the gas light and seemed especially keen to point of the miracle of the fires later lighting the veranda.

Given these unfortunate descriptions, perhaps the reader is concerned whether there was a proper

The Dinner Party

party at all. Did anyone speak with anyone? Did anyone listen to anyone? Well, that is what the Pimsleurs did. Mr Pimsleur and his daughters, Hildegard and Penelope, were the glue of the gathering; the leaven of the loaf. They each, in turn and in their own ways, made the community of the party rise to pleasant heights. Each guest, with their strange ways, was comfortable and made to feel so. Each guest was visited in rotation by Mr Pimsleur, by Hildegard Pimsleur, and by Penelope Pimsleur.

"How do you do, Mr Harold?" Mr Pimsleur said.

"I am quite well this evening, Mr Pimsleur. Thank you. And how do you doer?" Mr Harold said.

"Oh yes, well. Quite well. As well." Mr Pimsleur said. "Have you seen the plantings, Bruce?"

"Yes, Charles, I've seen the planterings- at least, the planterings on the north and east roads- I haven't been this way for some weeks." Mr Harold said. "They seem proper, though, do they not?"

"Certainly. Can I get you anything else, Bruce?" Mr Pimsleur said.

"No thank you, Fenton. Mrs Pimsleur is an exceptional hostess and I seem well-provisioned!" Mr Harold said.

"Thank you, Mr Harold!" The two men nodded cordially and Mr Pimsleur walked on.

Hildegard's turn was next.

"How do you do, Mr Harold?" Hildegard Pimsleur said.

"I am quite well this evening, Ms Pimsleur. Thank you. And how do you doess?" Mr Harold said.

"Oh. Quite well. As well." Hildegard said. "Have you seen the plantings, Mr Harold?"

"Yes, Ms Hildegard, I've seen the planterings- at least, the planterings on the north and east roads- I haven't been this way for some weeks." Mr Harold said. "They seem proper, though, do they not?"

"Certainly. Can I get you anything else, Mr Harold?" Hildegard said.

"No thank you, Ms Hildegard. Your mother is an exceptional hostess and I seem well-provisioned!" Mr Harold said.

"Thank you, Mr Harold!" Hildegard curtsied just enough and Mr Harold nodded cordially and Hildegard Pimsleur was on her way to the next guest.

Penelope's turn was next.

"How do you do, Mr Harold?" Penelope Pimsleur said.

"I am quite well this evening, Ms Pimsleur. Thank you. And how do you doess?" Mr Harold said.

"Oh. Quite well. As well." Penelope said. "Have you seen the plantings, Mr Harold?"

"Yes, Ms Penelope, I've seen the planterings- at least, the planterings on the north and east roads- I haven't been this way for some weeks." Mr Harold said. "They seem proper, though, do they not?"

"Certainly. Can I get you anything else, Mr Harold?" Penelope said.

The Dinner Party

"No thank you, Ms Penelope. Your mother is an exceptional hostess and I seem well-provisioned!" Mr Harold said.

"Thank you, Mr Harold!" Penelope curtsied perfectly and Mr Harold nodded cordially and Penelope Pimsleur was on her way to the next guest.

Amidst this swirling galaxy of guests and her family and the servants serving, Mrs Pimsleur was really in her element. Mr Harold was right; she was an exceptional hostess. Nothing was missing before it was found, nothing was lacking before it was provided, nothing was out of place before it was set right. She seemed to keep a mental list of anecdotes which each guest was capable of sharing when the sound of conversation threatened to stall, and she would call on each at just the right time. No one had to think of anything to say- Mrs Pimsleur could simply order up a story, anecdote or funny joke out of her head from any of the guests without hesitation.

Penelope was surprised to find herself just a little bored at dinner. She enjoyed the conversation- it was plain and easy to follow and there was no clever banter to decipher. She enjoyed dinner- cook was always excellent. But something was decidedly missing. She thought, at times throughout the evening, how terrible it would be if someone were to burglarise the house again while they were all together eating and distracted. She chided herself for entertaining such terrible thoughts but it led her down a path of thought which took her through a burglary, but ended with the brave constable, Caleb Cheswick on the scene and investigating- her elder by the insurmountable number of years of three- and she pictured him standing once again in the foyer, holding a manly conversation with her father and asking such mature and insightful questions as: "Mr Pimsleur, when did you notice the items were missing?" and "Where do you arrive home from?"

Yes, Caleb Cheswick was a particular riddle- perhaps even a riddle of strength and keen senses. What drive! What determination! What handsome features! How she wondered who would someday solve him!

"Ms Penelope?" Ms Blankenship said.

"Yes, Ms Blankenship?" Penelope said.

"Your mother informs me you have been tending the hydrangeas in the garden?" Ms Blankenship said.

"Oh, only a few- I am still learning." Penelope said.

"That is an excellent skill for a young lady to develop, if she plans to marry someday." Ms Blankenship said.

"Oh, I do plan to! That is, I don't have any definitive plans- to speak of- no true plan. But yes, I suppose a wife ought to know how to tend hydrangeas?" Penelope said.

"Oh, most certainly. Wouldn't you agree, Mrs Harold?" Ms Blankenship said.

The Dinner Party

"I'm sorry, my dearest, what was the question?" Mrs Harold said.

"I said, 'A young woman ought to know how to tend hydrangea if she plans to be married.' Isn't that right?" Ms Blankenship said.

"I suppose I have tended hydrangea. And I am married. I can see your point." Mrs Harold said. The connection was not too far-fetched for her mind to grasp. She was a Harold, after all.

"You see, Penelope? You are doing just the right thing by tending hydrangea." Ms Blankenship said.

Penelope struggled mightily whether to ask if Ms Blankenship tended hydrangea herself. She was certain it would be misconstrued, however, and restrained herself admirably. She thought of Hildegard. Hildegard was older. Why wasn't anyone speaking to Hildegard about marrying and tending hydrangea? Maybe they assumed she was already tending hydrangea and had plans to marry? Penelope decided to steer the conversation to a topic she had not only a personal connection with, but also a growing interest in.

"Has anyone seen Inspector Foxglove these past days?" Penelope said.

"Oh, dearess, that is certainly the question, isn't it?" Mrs Harold said.

Mr Rampert said nothing.

"I saw him! He was in my home- I hosted him." Mr Blankenship said.

"When did this happen, Mr Blankenship?" someone asked.

"Oh, quite recently." Mr Blankenship said.

"Just how recently, Mr Blankenship?" another asked.

"Perhaps four or five days ago. Not long at all!" Mr Blankenship said.

"Pardoner me, Mr Blankenship. I believe we have most all of us seen the Inspectorer quite recently. The subject at hand is, the relevant topic, is that no one seems to have seen him in two or three days." Mr Harold said.

The group spoke all at once concerning this for sometime and in the end agreed it had been between two and five days since anyone had seen him. Mr Rampert did not take part.

"And what of Constable Cheswick? Where has he been?" someone asked with earnest.

"He was at my house just recently." said Mr Blankenship. He felt it necessary to establish himself as being at the center of things, even if that meant associating himself with Cheswick momentarily.

"Was this also four or five days ago, Mr Blankenship?" Mr Harold said.

"Yes- quite so. He was with Inspector Foxglove. They were both in my house for tea, to discuss the recent crime wave." Mr Blankenship said.

"Yes, I believe we've established that fact, Mr Blankenship." Mr Harold said.

The Dinner Party

"To be sure. We had an excellent discussion." Mr Blankenship said. Mr Harold's veiled rebuttal did not seem to faze him in the least.

"I would like to say I did invite him tonight." Mrs Pimsleur said.

"Well, he ought to be here, then!" Mrs Harold said.

"Yes, certainly." Ms Blankenship said.

No one had heard a bell ring or heard a door knock, but suddenly, as if overhearing his name from across the county, Inspector Foxglove stood in the doorway of the dining room!

"Inspector Foxglove! You did receive my invitation!" Mrs Pimsleur said.

"No, madame. I did not. I have been away." Foxglove said. "Mr Pimsleur, are these your belongings, sir?"

Mr Pimsleur rose from his seat and came to the inspector and took the items he held out. Mr Pimsleur saw his own watch and cufflinks which had been stolen days earlier. He took a surprised step back.

"Inspector Foxglove! Those are my watch and cufflinks! Where did you find them?" Mr Pimsleur said.

"I went south to Brakton. I found a peddler there who directed me to a beggar who directed me to a shut-in aristocrat who told me about a pawn shop. I entered the pawn shop and instantly spotted these items. When I inquired of the pawnbroker, he informed me these were new items, only recently brought in. I purchased them- a price for my first substantial clue!" Foxglove said.

"A clue! A clue to what, Inspector?"

"My first clue as to who is behind the robberies!" said Inspector Foxglove.

12 THE WOOING OF MISS PENELOPE PIMSLEUR BY MR NILES BLANKENSHIP

In Which Mr Niles Blankenship Attempts to Woo Miss Penelope Pimsleur

The appearance of Inspector Foxglove at the Pimsleur party had startled everyone. Each sat- or half stood- in their place, watching as Mr Pimsleur had identified his belongings, and listening as Foxglove explained how he had found them in a pawn shop in Brakton and how it pointed him- via a long and difficult line of reasoning which, though it sounded perfectly obvious while he explained it no one could follow, and afterward, no one could recall- to the notorious Orton Black as the culprit of the crimes which had been committed.

The name of Orton Black had not meant anything to anyone at the party, and thus the impact was perhaps lessened thereby, but when Inspector Foxglove regaled them with his tale of his pursuit of Orton Black and the near misses he had had in his attempts to apprehend him, they all marveled at the Inspector's fortitude and resolve. His determination and cunning in identifying Orton Black was astonishing to all.

Inspector Foxglove then spoke to them all, warning them to be on their guard. To be vigilant to the utmost. Orton Black, he said, Orton Black is a nefarious criminal and a master of many disguises. Be watchful of anyone in town or on the moor you do not recognise. Be cautious of anyone you see engaged in anything other than routine activity. Be mindful of anyone who has only recently arrived in Westwich whom you do not recognise.

"I have been chasing this Orton Black for a number of years now. No one but myself really knows what he looks like- and I have only seen him in passing; a fleeting glance is all! We must not suspect everyone- but we must be doubly and triply cautious now that I have identified him." Foxglove said.

"But Inspector, the crimes have already been committed! The thief has already gone- he has sold our things in Brakton! Why should we be on our guard here in Westwich?"

"That is an excellent question. I must tell you about Orton Black. He is no ordinary criminal. He will not be content with a few crimes- troubling though they may be to you, it is only part of a larger game with him. I must confess, I believe it is my very pursuit of him which has brought him here. I believe he plans to embarrass me in front of you. He desires an audience- the larger the better! And what better audience than the entire village of Westwich? He will attempt something unexpected and diabolical to defeat me as you look on." Foxglove said.

The weight of this strange situation lay heavily upon them all. A famous detective and a notorious criminal engaged in a cat and mouse game in their midst. Their own village would be the scene of the ultimate showdown between the champion of the law and the master criminal.

Foxglove still held their attention.

"Good citizens of Westwich, do not fear. I am Inspector Foxglove and this Orton Black will not prevail. He has extended his hand so far he cannot draw it back. He has put himself in his own noose and I will bring him to a swift and definite justice!" Foxglove said.

This brought a rousing applause from that gathering and their hearts were lightened. Foxglove dismissed himself and the guests talked about the great turn of events and revelations of the evening.

Penelope Pimsleur found herself sitting quietly on a stone bench at the edge of the veranda, then she was suddenly not alone.

"Ms Penelope." Mr Blankenship said.

"Oh, Mr Blankenship." Penelope said. She rose.

"Please, I couldn't help overhearing at dinner that you have begun tending the hydrangeas?" Mr Blankenship said.

"Yes. I have. Only a few. I am still learning." Penelope said.

"That is an admirably task for a young lady to learn." Mr Blankenship said.

"So I have heard, Mr Blankenship." Penelope said. For the life of her, Penelope could not understand why Mr Blankenship would have anything to say to her or about the hydrangeas. He puzzled her more when he spoke again.

"May I see the hydrangeas?" Mr Blankenship said.

"Of course, Mr Blankenship. They are just over there, beyond the veranda. You see them beside the garden wall?" Penelope said. "It is well lit there, even at night."

Mr Blankenship smiled.

"Ms Penelope, would you please show me the hydrangeas? I do not know enough about them to know what I am looking at. Perhaps you could assist me in my appreciation of them?" Mr Blankenship said.

"Of course, Mr Blankenship." Penelope said.

They walked together to the garden wall beyond the veranda where the hydrangeas were in blossom; Penelope with her hands folded in front of her, Blankenship with his hands folded behind his back.

"These are the hydrangeas, Mr Blankenship." Penelope said. This was becoming a very strange conversation for her. It would become stranger still.

Mr Blankenship appeared to observe the hydrangeas very closely.

"How many hydrangeas are there? I mean, how many plants is this?" Mr Blankenship said.

"These are three here. There are more within the garden wall." Penelope said.

"They are as pretty as you, Miss Penelope." Mr Blankenship said.

"I find them smelly. And too full to be very attractive." Penelope said.

"They are fragrant! Surely you think they are fragrant?!" Mr Blankenship said.

"I'm afraid I don't, Mr Blankenship. I do not enjoy caring for them because I do not particularly like the smell. I much prefer roses." Penelope said.

"I see." Mr Blankenship said.

They observed the hydrangeas silently for a while.

"Miss Pimsleur. As you know, I am quite wealthy. My estate is the largest second on the moor- second only on the moor to your own father's estate. I have a garden, too. And you could plant roses there if you like." Mr Blankenship said.

Penelope interrupted.

"Mr Blankenship, I think I would plant roses here first. I do not need to plant in your garden. But I thank you for your offer, I suppose." Penelope said.

"You misunderstand me. I am proposing you plant roses in your own garden." Mr Blankenship said.

"I thank you for the advice. I will speak to my mother about planting some roses here. Yes. I think that would be very nice." Penelope said.

Mr Blankenship's hands seemed to be further behind his back than before.

"No. Miss Pimsleur, I am proposing a marriage. My garden would become your garden and you could then plant roses in our garden to your heart's content (you will check with me before doing so, of course). I will make you the most envied and elegant lady in all of Westwich and beyond- I will make you Mrs Niles Blankenship! You will come and make my garden your own garden- our garden, in truth. I would still have to approve your plans for the garden." Mr Blankenship said.

We must now say two things. One, the reader must not dim their view of Penelope for not seeing this proposal coming and her inability to grasp it at the outset or at least anticipate it. She was not slow or dull or flighty- the truth is that the idea of Niles Blankenship proposing was the furthest thing from the moon. It was quite literally, and entirely, unexpected.

We must also say, for Mr Blankenship's sake, that this was by far not the worst proposal in the history of the village of Westwich. We hate to admit it, but this was actually better than average for that neighborhood.

"Mr Blankenship, are you proposing to me?" Penelope said.

"My dear Penelope, who else would I be proposing to?" Mr Blankenship said.

"Surely there is someone else?" Penelope said. She meant it one way, he took it the other.

"I suppose there might be, but I am proposing to you!" Mr Blankenship said.

"Mr Blankenship. I don't know what to say." Penelope said.

"I can give you some words, if you like." Mr Blankenship said.

"I am sorry, Mr Blankenship. May I have a moment to collect my thoughts?" Penelope said.

"Of course." Mr Blankenship said.

"I don't need a moment, but I thank you. Mr Blankenship, marriage is not in my contemplation at this time in my young life and because it is not in my contemplation, I cannot contemplate marrying you." Penelope said.

"Why, Miss Penelope, you don't need to contemplate it. You must only say 'Yes.' There is no contemplation required!" Mr Blankenship said.

"I thank you for your kind offer of, of proposing, but I must refuse you. Thank you again. Good evening, Mr Blankenship." Penelope said.

"I see." said Mr Blankenship.

Penelope watched him walk abruptly back to the veranda and speak quickly and quietly with his sister. She glanced in Penelope's direction with a fire which seemed to leap out across the veranda. The siblings turned as one and, without saying goodbye to the Pimsleurs or anyone else, strode back into the house and, as expected, left for home without another word.

"So that is what it is like." Penelope said to herself.

Hildegard was instantly at Penelope's side.

"Pen, what happened? He looked as though he might explode!" Hildegard said.

"Oh, Hilde! He proposed!" Penelope said. And now the weight of it all manifested itself and she sank into her sister's arms.

"Dear Pen! I hope you did not accept, if that was his response!" Hildegard said.

"No. No I did not. I am sure I said no." Penelope said.

"Are you quite sure?" Hildegard said.

"Yes, yes quite sure." Penelope said. "Hilde, he said uncomfortable things about hydrangeas and roses and gardens and, and marriage!"

"Shh. My little Pen. He is gone and he has taken his proposal and his awful sister with him." Hildegard said.

"OH! What if I had accidentally said yes, Hilde! What if I had unintentionally become her sister-in-law! I am in horror!" Penelope said.

"You are safe, Pen. You said no." Hildegard said- then gave a startled sound. "You did say no, didn't you?"

"Of course I did." Penelope said, though it brought her little comfort.

Mrs Pimsleur would remember it as the most exciting party she had given in a very long time.

***

The breakfast table at the Pimsleur household the next morning was full of unusual conversations. The party had its own charms, but the sudden appearance of Inspector Foxglove coupled with the shocking and unexpected proposal of Mr Niles Blankenship had given the family- not to mention the surrounding neighborhood- enough to talk about for weeks, let alone a quaint family breakfast. This was all well and good for news-mongers, but the Pimsleurs were particularly affected by it all. It was, after all, their own Penelope who had refused the unexpected proposal and it was Mr Pimsleur himself who had identified his stolen belongings when Foxglove presented them in such dramatic fashion. These artifacts taken together were altogether too much and the family sat wedged in between the topics.

Mrs Pimsleur knew that talking was the solution and Mr Pimsleur instinctively understood silence was key. Penelope answered what questions she could and Hildegard deflected as many as were asked to either her sister or father.

When they heard the knock at the door, it was unexpected to say the least.

It was announced that Mr Niles Blankenship wished to speak with Mr Pimsleur.

Mr Pimsleur excused himself, eyeing Penelope as he set his napkin down. He left the room to meet Mr Blankenship and found him in the sitting room, placid and composed. Mr Blankenship appeared thoughtful and at the sight of him in that repose, Mr Pimsleur realized he had never seen Blankenship in that manner and, come to think of it, it did not suit him well. The guest rose.

"Mr Pimsleur, how do you do sir? I must speak with you." Mr Blankenship said.

"I am at your disposal, Mr Blankenship." Mr Pimsleur said.

"Good. I am here to speak with you about your daughter, Penelope. I have, for some time, given consideration to the prospect of marriage- my own, of course- and Ms Pimsleur has largely been the object of those considerations. It occurs to me that before I speak to her on the matter, I ought to, out of courtesy, respect and tradition, speak with you on the issue and fathom your mind regarding the possibility of my proposal." Mr Blankenship said.

The Wooing of Miss Penelope Pimsleur

Mr Pimsleur continued his policy of silence, carried over from the breakfast table.

"My proposal to your daughter, of course, is not one of mere feeling and expressions of devotion- it is a statement of fiduciary partnership. A proposal, from me, would be a high sign for Ms Pimsleur, an omen of good fortune and not only an omen- it would be a firm reality. I have a fortune similar to your own and the joining of our households would strengthen each of our standings in the neighborhood and in the wider world." Mr Blankenship said.

Mr Pimsleur continued his policy of silence. He did not have the choice now.

"Far be it from me to marry a foreigner or a poor woman from another town and bring her here to Westwich (we have the future to think about, Mr Pimsleur). And imagine the catastrophe- I shudder- imagine your own Penelope marrying a traveling gypsy who may perhaps claim to be a prince of his people but of course all that really means is that he has more chickens than will fit in his carriage house. This, sir, is not what the citizens of highest standing in the neighborhood want or deserve. No sir. We do not. We deserve the very best marriages of convenience, of beauty and of fiscal strength." Mr Blankenship said.

"I cannot stress enough the aspect of strength, the prospect of combining our holdings, ultimately, and what that would mean for our fortunes. It would give us access to higher investments, to greater opportunities, to all those things which are withheld from us- even in our current stations. You seek, as do I, the expansion of my kingdom and I see the two of us, meeting together like this, as two kings of old Britannia- and I extend my golden torc to you in good faith and in well-wishing. I propose- not merely a marriage, no- I propose a great and glorious kingdom."

Mr Pimsleur was not a harsh man, it should be said. But he had a harsh thought once in a while and he was suppressing one just now.

"Mr Blankenship. Forgive me. I believe you have already spoken to my daughter." Mr Pimsleur said.

Blankenship waved him off. "No. No. I, I broached the subject to gauge her understanding of the possibility. I needed to know if she could grasp what I was offering." Mr Blankenship said.

"Mr Blankenship, I am fairly certain you directly proposed marriage to my daughter. Is that right?" Mr Pimsleur said.

"Yes. I certainly did. I realised my mistake last night and came here to rectify it first thing. Clearly, I was in error and needed to speak with you first. So, here I am- good to my word." Mr Blankenship said. He spread his hands as evidence he was good to his word. We might mention those hands were quite empty.

"I am not sure I quite follow. You speak as if speaking to my daughter last night was an error. I see no error in it- at least, not in the fact of speaking to her first." Mr Pimsleur said.

"Ah, I see your point. But, you notice, she did not accept my proposal. This is what made me reconsider. So, I have come to you instead." Mr Blankenship.

"Plainly, you have come to me. What can I give you that Penelope did not?" Mr Pimsleur.

"Nearly right- just the opposite! Your daughter did not accept my proposal but you, in your better sense and judgement can accept on her behalf. It is clearly the right match- surely you see that?" Mr Blankenship said. He smiled the broad smile of one who threatens.

"For the sake of clarity, then: you did not receive the answer you desired from my daughter and you are asking me to override her refusal and give my consent as if it were her own?" Mr Pimsleur.

Mr Blankenship affected to take a step back and spoke his next words with great admiration. "That is masterfully spoken, Mr Pimsleur. Yes, that is precisely why I am here. I knew I was in the right to do so." Mr Blankenship said.

"Well, I will not give you what my daughter has already refused, Mr Blankenship. That is not the way of things anymore." Mr Pimsleur said. "I hope you have something else to discuss or I am afraid you only wasted a fine morning by coming here."

Back in the breakfast room, Mrs Pimsleur and her girls ate in silence and up to this point in the elapsation of time, had heard no portion of the conversation. But now they plainly heard the unchristian language of Mr Niles Blankenship pour forth in vacillation of intelligible and unintelligible, spurts of eloquence and doggerel and all the while sustained at such a terrific volume of decibels that even the cook- herself a woman of no mean talent concerning crude verbiage- probably learned a few things to add to her vocabulary.

13 ON THE HEELS OF ORTON BLACK

In Which Inspector Foxglove and Constable Cheswick Transfer the Case

The disappearance and reemergence of Inspector Foxglove had Westwich talking for days and left Cheswick quite at a loss as to what to do while the inspector was missing. He thought briefly about the possibility of a Missing Persons Report but felt, surely, the District wouldn't take him seriously if he reported their top man had walked out into the night and disappeared without a word. Perhaps a Missing Persons Report Under Special Circumstances would have done the trick, but these were not procedures which Messrs Greene and Finchley went into much detail on in their excellent little handbook and left too many questions for Cheswick to adequately pursue it.

This created a dilemma for Cheswick. Could he still pursue the investigation on his own terms? He began to see what they meant when they talked about being left "in the lurch"- it was not a phrase that meant any sense to him, but he decided the feeling was nonetheless accurate. Of equally pressing importance in Cheswick's mind: Did the disappearance of Foxglove mean that the imposed moratorium on speaking his intentions to Penelope Pimsleur was lifted? Another result of the interim period was Cheswick's clarity regarding Ms Penelope Pimsleur. He had determined that, should everything with the case allow, he would approach Ms Pimsleur and discuss his hope of attachment.

He spent the better part of those days fruitlessly reviewing the case and ranging the countryside. Had anyone asked him what he was doing ranging the countryside, he likely would have told them he was looking for Inspector Foxglove but much more likely, he was back to his botanical habits. Like Adam before him, he sought to hide himself from his troubles in the trees, and in Cheswick's case, pretend to study them.

The third day out, inexplicable to anyone who might have been paying attention, Cheswick went to the telegraph office and sent off a dispatch. Maybe it was because Inspector Foxglove was nowhere to be seen. Perhaps it was because the investigation seemed to have come to a halt. He was in and out of the office quickly and anyone would have thought he had actually gone into the wrong door and abruptly left, immediately realizing his mistake. But that day, Cheswick meant to go into the telegraph office send off a brief note and this he did.

Thus, when Inspector Foxglove returned, Constable Cheswick was finally able to see his way forward. Foxglove insisted they visit next Ms Williams. "Let us see how our visit with the Williams household goes." he said, "It may tell us something more than we know."

It did. But not what Foxglove seemed to be hoping for. They sat with Ms Williams for nearly fifteen minutes before Foxglove mentioned the robbery. Ms Williams recounted, nearly word for word what she had told Cheswick- her memory seemed quite intact. Then Foxglove pursued the question of the vagrant hooligan.

"Ms Williams, we have heard some rumor of a stranger in town." He gave her the description other had given him. "Have you seen this man about your property?"

"Yes, I've certainly seen him, Inspector." Ms Williams said.

"Perhaps he was came to your door looking for work? Or begging? Or wanted to rent a room, perhaps?" Foxglove said.

"Of course he wanted something. And I, of course, gave him whatever he asked!" Ms Williams said!

Foxglove became very concerned suddenly. "Ms Williams! This man is a suspect! We have reason to believe this man is the thief and burglar that stole your candlesticks and has robbed four others houses in the neighbourhood!"

"Suspect! Oh my!" Ms Williams said. Her happy countenance had disappeared.

"Madame, do you know anything about his whereabouts?" Foxglove said.

"I know where he is, if that is what you mean." Ms Williams said. "He is upstairs."

"Upstairs! At this very moment?!" Foxglove said. He leaped to his feet, and Cheswick with him.

"Yes, I'll show you his room." Ms Williams said.

"NO! Please sit down again. The Constable and I will take care of this." Foxglove motioned for Cheswick to follow. "Which room is his, Ms Williams?"

She pointed. "Up those stairs, then left, then the stairs on the right. The second door up there. You'll see it."

"Steady, Constable. We will approach him quietly and take him unawares. Softly now." Foxglove said, as they began the ascent up the first stair. They took slow steps with their boots on the carpet runner, so the minute creaks did not give them away. After what felt like a long time, they came up the second stair and were at the second door.

Foxglove and Cheswick made eye contact and the detective inspector began counting off silently with his fingers- on 'three', they both burst into the room. There was no one in sight. Merely a rumpled bed, a few things laid out from an overnight bag. But the window was open and the sheer curtain wafted in the breeze.

"He went out the window?" Cheswick said. He raced to the ledge and looked out, there was no place for a man to go out that window. It was a three meter drop to a steeply sloped roof below. He leaned out- was there something to grab hold of up above?

"I don't see anything, Inspector." Cheswick said.

Foxglove was silent, looking about the room intently. His arms were crossed and his eyebrows furrowed.

Suddenly, they heard Ms Williams shout from downstairs. The two men exchanged a look of alarm and raced off back down the stairs, giving no heed to their noise now. The sitting room they had left Ms Williams in was empty and they called out for her.

"In here, Inspector! He's in the kitchen, Constable!" they heard her say.

They entered the kitchen and found Ms Williams smiling, and pointing. They followed her point to the small kitchen table where a man- perfectly fitting the description of the vagrant hooligan- sat eating a small loaf and some cheese. He was in mid bite.

"Stay where you are, sir!" Foxglove shouted. "Who are you?"

Ms Williams answered for the man who was still chewing.

"He's my son, Inspector." she said "But now I think about it, he can't have been the burglar. He's been with me every evening."

"Ms Williams," Constable Cheswick said "Not to be indelicate, but you said plainly you had no children, and now you say our prime suspect is your son?"

"Oh, yes, he's certainly my son. But he doesn't care much for candelabras." Ms Williams said.

"Ms Williams. That is not an explanation." Foxglove said sternly.

"Gentlemen, if I may?" the man at the table had finished chewing and was now standing. He was dressed like a gentleman and his manner was pleasant, but direct. The turned their attention to him. "My mother is right. I am her son- but I have been gone a very long time. She had lost hope I might come back. It seems none of my telegrams ever reached her but now I am here."

"That is curious timing, sir; we are in the midst of a crime wave and you are the only newcomer anyone has noticed these past few weeks." Cheswick said.

"I cannot explain the coincidence but I can assure you it is a coincidence. I will put you in touch with people- upstanding people in London, or Birmingham, or Glasgow- who can vouch for me. I am an attache, or was, to the crown prince

He says it only confirms his suspicions further. Their interview with Ms Williams was unexpected in that she was able to identify the vagrant hooligan- her son, long missing and now returned! Cheswicks remarks it is a letdown and they are now back to the beginning of the investigation, as it were. Foxglove corrects him to the understanding that it narrows the field even more. He elaborates:

"Constable, I think I can confidently say we can now wrap this case up." Foxglove said. They were sitting at the pub again.

"That is good news, I think, but what do you mean? Doesn't wrapping up a case mean we have the criminal behind bars? I thought that wrapping up a case meant doing the final paperwork?" Cheswick said.

"No." Foxglove said. He laughed. "It simply means the end of the investigation for you. You have handed me the case in completion and I will take it from here. I will maintain my base of operations in your office, but I must now go out into the highways and byways to bring the criminal in. He left me a clew in Brakton- most likely to throw me off the track- but we will investigate it nonetheless. In fact…"

Foxglove eyed Cheswick carefully.

"Constable, you are officially finished with the investigation, but I think I will send you to Brakton to conclude our investigation there. One last task. How would that be?" Foxglove said.

"I? I don't know. If you told me, I suppose, what to do then I could do it." Cheswick said.

"Oh, it will be entirely routine, I assure you." Foxglove said. "Nothing you haven't already done admirably here in Westwich. I do not think the thief will even be there now. I suspect he has gone north or east now. I will send you south to Brakton and keep you quite safe."

"Will no one be here?" Cheswick said.

"What?" Foxglove said.

"Will no one be here? Do you intend to send us both away while Orton Black is on the loose?" Cheswick said.

"No. Of course not. I will stay while you go down to Brakton and when you return, I will make my rounds. That means, of course, that you must get down there and back quite quickly. We haven't time for dawdling." Foxglove said.

Cheswick nodded.

"I can leave as soon as you say." Cheswick said.

"You should leave first thing tomorrow morning and be back by evening. Mr Cheswick, I would also like to speak freely regarding Ms Pimsleur and our earlier conversation regarding my concerns in connection with your feelings for her." Foxglove said.

"Yes?" Cheswick said.

Foxglove smiled. "I think you may now speak freely with Ms Pimsleur. Our charade will not fool Orton Black so there is no reason to keep it up. I give you my blessing!" Foxglove said. He made a show of crossing Cheswick with his mug in hand and spilled just a little.

Cheswick was quite frozen. "Inspector. Do you know that Niles Blankenship has already proposed to her?" Cheswick said.

"That is the rumour, isn't it?" Foxglove said.

"I think it is more than a rumour." Cheswick said.

"Well, nevertheless, she is not so foolish as to marry such an imbecile as Blankenship. I daresay the way is clear for you." Foxglove said. "Further, I have spoken with the District and made a recommendation. If you chose to stay here in Westwich, rather than going back to university, they would make you their permanent Constable- with a generous enough salary that you could speak to Ms Pimsleur without hesitation. Between your inheritance and a constable's salary, you could live out your lives quite comfortably right here in your native home."

"Inspector Foxglove, you have become a patron overnight!" Cheswick said. "Why this change of heart?"

"It is no change of heart, Mr Cheswick. You have established yourself as a capable man of the law and I have certainly never been against your desired union with Ms Pimsleur- I only needed you to wait a bit while we sorted out this case. I am quite in favor of it, though I really have no personal connection to it." Foxglove said.

"No personal connection?! You have made it possible by your own personal influence. I daresay it is personal!" Cheswick said.

"Perhaps. Yes, I suppose it is personal, Mr Cheswick." Foxglove said. "I am on the very heels of Orton Black now!"

So by the end of that very week, the case was nearly solved and Mr Caleb Cheswick was engaged to Ms Penelope Pimsleur.

14 THE FIRE WHICH CONSUMES

In Which the Fortune of the Pimsleur Family is Tragically and Entirely Lost

On June the 7th, 1883, a tragedy occurred at the Pimsleur estate which will shape the rest of this story and make everything, which only a moment ago seemed so easy and obvious, very difficult.

In brief, that morning of June 7th, a fire broke out in one of the outbuildings of the Pimsleur farm, catching hold of some dry hay (the spring rained being seemingly delayed), and it began to feed on the one small building., both gorging itself and developing its appetite. It devoured the entire shack in an inferno and in that dry spring the fire spread rapidly from there across the estate- by the end, no building was spared, no winter wheat untouched, no structure, no single hydrangea or other recognisable feature remained of what was once the grand and beautiful Pimsleur estate. And though the family and various staff and hands of the estate were spared, there was also much loss of livestock and poultry.

The smoke of that fire could be seen from all four corners of the moor and Westwich proper. It became known, in the months following, as the Pimsleur Fire and the entire county saw the smoke of it and even down in Brakton, they had a sampling of ash dust on the buildings which faced the direction of the fire.

The Pimsleur family moved to temporary rooms in Westwich proper, above the Bull and Ox- the four of them huddled in smaller quarters than they knew what to do in. Their loyal servants and hands retired to families and connections across the county. Indeed, the tragedy of the Pimsleur estate had not only put them out of a home, but those they employed now represented a wave of unemployment a small town like Westwich could hardly absorb. Their housekeeper began commercing back and forth from Westwich to her sister's in the next county- she would not be dissuaded.

The fortunes of the Pimsleur had instantly changed and the fire likely made the future happiness of the Pimsleur family impossible- and even if they did struggle and find some measure of happiness, it would surely be small indeed?

As regards our story up to this point, we may briefly say that Constable Cheswick had gone to Brakton on Foxglove's orders and found nothing of note. Upon his return, Inspector Foxglove immediately left for his investigative rounds in other towns and was many miles away when a telegram arrived at his hotel lodgings informing him of the Pimsleur fire.

Mr Niles Blankenship- the closest thing to a villian we have encountered yet in this story- now made a visit to the temporary lodging of the Pimsleur family. He knocked on the door assigned to the family and set his face in a mask of disdain for the shabbiness of their situation. He had long coveted the Pimsleur estate for his own and the disdain he worn now, he often use to wear in mock of his own home when he compared it to the Pimsleurs'. But now that the Pimsleur estate was a broken and burnt pile of rubble, the Blankenship house and land were the finest in the neighborhood. It was on this pretense of new-found superiority that Mr Niles Blankenship felt at liberty to look down on the situation of his once perceived-rival.

As we said, Niles Blankenship knocked at the door and was resolved to be disdainful, and when Mr Pimsleur opened the door, Mr Blankenship succeeded in his communication of disdain.

"Mr Blankenship." said Mr Pimsleur.

"Mr Pimsleur." said Mr Blankenship. "I have come to offer my condolences. It was a beautiful house."

Mr Pimsleur said nothing. He patiently waited for the other to fill his own vacuum. Which Mr Blankenship was quick to do.

"I have a deep sympathy and a genuine heart to help those in my community who have fallen on troubled times. It's quite apparent to me that no one in our neighborhood has fallen on such troubled and desperate times as your own. I reach out my hand- only symbolically, of course- to a man I once viewed as a peer. I don't want to rub it in, so to speak, because I am sensitive to the human condition. I have come to offer you a position of employment. I cannot offer much of a salary- but I have spoken to my managers and we can fit you into our limited budgets on a modest sum. It may be taxing work and less than you are used to as an income. But it will be something. It will be a job. Certainly, that is worth something? The satisfaction at the end of each day, knowing you have contributed to society? Perhaps it is only raking leaves and cleaning twigs out of the driveway- but for god's sake, Mr Pimsleur, I am offering you dignity!"

This last word of Mr Blankenship's, 'dignity', was spoken to the door which Mr Pimsleur had slowly begun closing when Mr Blankenship had begun talking about the human condition. Mr Blankenship raised his voice and offered one, final word of common sense: "Dignity!" he said. He went back out to his phaeton and rode home, feeling he had done all he could do for an obstinate and troubled man.

Then the Pimsleurs had another visitor. Caleb Cheswick had gone to see Penelope in the new rooms in Westwich and been turned away at the door by her father.

"You see our condition, Mr Cheswick. Our situation is impossible and my daughter can no longer accept the proposal you made. To accept it now would simply be charity." Mr Pimsleur said.

"But sir, she accepted prior to your change of situation! And I do not rescind my offer!" Cheswick said.

"You must accept this change of events, Mr Cheswick. As we are." Mr Pimsleur said. "I am sorry. Truth is, I do not think she could bear to see you yet. It is difficult enough."

Returning bewildered to his rooms, Cheswick found a note left for him. Inspector Foxglove had returned that morning and asked him to meet him immediately on the North Bridge and, rather mysteriously, insisted he not be seen or followed to their meeting place. He was already dressed and so, without even ascending to his rooms, Cheswick went right back out the door toward the South Bridge, thinking to cut back across the fields to the North Bridge once he was out of town. He thought Foxglove would approve of this perambulation.

As he walked, he turned over and over in his mind the change of his fortune with Penelope. Just days ago, they had been happy and engaged- not marrying for money, but now realizing that money made it possible. The Pimsleur fire had changed his own life as well as their own. He understood the position of marrying out of poverty- Penelope would only be seen as accepting charity and it would undermine her character to do so.

He cut now from the road leading south and back across the fields to the North Bridge. From a distance he saw no one on the bridge but Foxglove had spotted him and appeared briefly out of the shadows to surreptitiously wave at him, then melded back into hiding.

This gave Cheswick tremendous pause. He cast a long look behind him to be sure he was not followed and only proceeded when he felt confident he was alone. He took now a circuitous route from that spot to the bridge, tracking along the riverbank to avoid the road even further. He stopped in a close gathering of trees and Foxglove joined him, well away from the bridge.

"Good man." Foxglove said. "You have more of the detective in you than you know!"

"Inspector, what is this all about? Have you found something about Orton Black?" Cheswick said.

They were speaking in whispers, even here in the trees.

The Fire Which Consumes

"I sincerely hope that what I have found does not lead us back to Orton Black, Constable. That would be dire news indeed." Foxglove said.

"So you have found something! What is it? The suspense and secrecy of this-" Cheswick said.

"I must ask you a few questions first, to confirm my suspicions?" Foxglove said.

"Yes. Please. If that is all that hinders you!" Cheswick said.

"First, what brand of cigar do you smoke?" Foxglove said.

"Inspector, I smoke cigars, but I do not think I have told anyone that I do. I smoke only on my walks afar." Cheswick said. Then he answered the question. "I smoke a brand called Herrington."

Foxglove nodded solemnly. He produced from his pocket a handkerchief and unwrapped it. In the open handkerchief was a cigar butt- just a stub but the distinctive stub of a Herrington brand cigar. Cheswick gave a start when he saw this.

"Second, when you proposed to Ms Pimsleur, were you wearing those boots?" Foxglove said.

"Yes. These boots. Inspector, what is this?" Cheswick said.

"If the heel of your left boot worn away on the one side?" Foxglove said.

"I don't know." Cheswick said. Foxglove was already on his knee in the grass, lifting the boot. Cheswick steadied himself with his hand on a tree.

"The answer is yes." Foxglove said. He was very grim now. "Thirdly, Constable. Is this yours?" And Foxglove produced from his other pocket a copy of Messrs Green and Finchley's *Manual of Dutief And Functionf Of A Constable: a Handbook*. It was singed at the edges

"No. Inspector, that is not mine! Thankfully, I have my copy here in my-" Cheswick said. But as he reached for it in his coat pocket, he stopped. "Inspector. My manual is missing. How did you get this?"

"Constable." Foxglove said. He was very serious. "I found these items at the scene of the Pimsleur fire. Next to a very careful impression of your boot in the soft dirt near the woodline of the main house yard."

Cheswick stared dumbly at him.

"Constable, this is all evidence of arson." Foxglove said.

"Arson? There was no arson, only an accident." Cheswick said.

"No, Constable. There was most certainly arson committed. Did you investigate it as arson?" Foxglove said.

"Inspector, you don't think I would have- that I could even consider such a thing!" Cheswick said. "I see this is all evidence against me- but I did not!"

"I know you did not. I'm afraid someone has decided to frame you for the crime, Constable. I know perfectly well you didn't do it. We have in our advantage the fact that the perpetrator likely doesn't know you were in love with Ms Pimsleur and had actually proposed to her or he would never have tried to point the investigation at you. I thought these were your things when I saw them and wanted to ask you privately first." Foxglove said.

"I am in your debt, Inspector, for believing me. What should we do now?" Cheswick said.

"It is a difficult question, Constable. We must ascertain two things. One, was this a separate crime from the robberies or is this also part of Orton Black's scheme? And secondly, did he have an accomplice in Westwich? But I believe I have a solution to both." Foxglove said.

"What solution could you possibly offer that covers all of that, Inspector?" Cheswick said.

"I need you to do something for me." Foxglove said.

***

A few hours after Foxglove and Westwich had their secret meeting near the North bridge, word began to spread around Westwich of a Town Meeting to be held that Thursday night to update citizens on the progress of the investigation into the recent burglaries and to address the tragic fire at the Pimsleur Estate.

That Thursday night, Inspector Foxglove- clearly in charge of the meeting- addressed the town. "It pains me to inform you that the recent tragedy at the Pimsleur Estate was, I am afraid, not an accident."

Gasps.

"That's right. It is my difficult duty to inform you the fire which destroyed the home and property of the Pimsleur family was deliberately, and expertly, set by someone. At this time, I believe they acted alone. I must now name the arsonist. His name is Caleb Cheswick, (there was a scream from the crowd) formerly the constable of this town and a man who is now a desperate criminal and on the run from the law. He is most certainly gone from the immediate area and likely is seeking refuge far from here. He undoubtedly knows by now that I have investigated the scene and he is most certainly missing from his person the items which I now have in my possession which are definitive proof of his intention and guilt in the deplorable act of arson."

Penelope Pimsleur did not hear anything the Inspector said after she heard Caleb Cheswick named as the arsonist. The scream which briefly interrupted Foxglove was followed by the sound of sobbing, footsteps and skirts as Penelope abruptly let the church. In their shock, no one blamed or followed her out the door, excepting her sister who only followed her without blame.

What Inspector Foxglove said next was only communicated to her later.

"Ladies and Gentlemen. In my career of law, I have come up against only one man who has successfully eluded me. That man's name is Orton Black. I have sufficient evidence to convince me that the name Orton Black is merely an alias and not his true name. Not only is it an alias, it is an alias used by none other than Caleb Cheswick. That's right. I can with near-certainty tell you publicly that the notorious criminal Orton Black and Caleb Cheswick are one and the same.

"In case you doubt, let me enumerate the following points of proof to my assertion and conclusion. One! Caleb Cheswick was the son of a man of law like myself. As such, he suffered exposure from a young age to the world of criminality and likely heard its siren call at that young age. Two! As the son of a man of law, he would have known the ways of the police- like breathing or like a second language. His ability to naturally anticipate and evade the law comes of this environment. Three! His career in university studying biology is entirely unconfirmed by the university itself- they have no knowledge or record of any such person as Caleb Cheswick ever, I repeat, ever, attending their university. Four! That same interval of years in which he claimed to have been away studying is the very same interval of years in which I first came upon the crimes of Orton Black- that is no coincidence!

"I surmise this, that Caleb Cheswick, having full knowledge of the law and of crime, began to form a plan in his devious mind from a young age. That he deliberately left this town for London, under the pretense of study, and instead immersed himself in the seemy underworld of crime and vice in that noble city. There, under the assumed name of Orton Black, began a nefarious career and has decided, coinciding with his father's death, to bring his terrible acts here to Westwich, thinking he, the mighty criminal, could fool all of you- you who thought you knew him so well!- and take from under your noses your valuables and possession as if it were a game to be played with children!"

By the time Inspector Foxglove had finished this speech, the entire neighbourhood of Westwich might have been on fire, so hot was the indignation and rising fury of the citizens as they heard one of their own had been the instigator of not only the burglaries which had so upset them all but an arsonist as well.

"But what of proof, Inspector? What proof do you have of these accusations? Are we really to believe all this? Are we to simply take your (respected, no doubt) word? How are we to know Mr Cheswick started that fire? What evidence can there be? It was most plainly an accident- a tragic, tragic accident, surely?" someone said.

"I understand and admire your reluctance to accept the betrayal of one of your own. My years in the relentless enforcement of our laws has, perhaps, hardened me to the prospect of innocence. I look for guilt first, and innocence after. But in this case, even I find myself moved. It is with great remorse I produce these evidences."

And with those words, Foxglove reached into one pocket and held up the Constable's Handbook,

"This is, with his own notes in his own handwriting, the Constable's Handbook belonging to Caleb Cheswick. I found this on the property, near the edges of the clearing."

Then Foxglove reached his other hand into his other pocket and held up, in a clean, white hankerchief, the butt end of one of Cheswick's cigars.

"And this, confirmed to be Caleb Cheswick's favorite pet brand of cigar- difficult to find in these counties- which he used to start the fire at the Pimsleur Estate."

Gasps and shouts. No one knew Cheswick was a smoker.

"I must ask quite candidly, has anyone here ever participated or observed such an investigation as the one we are about to conduct here in Westwich?" No one raised a hand or indicated any knowledge whatsoever of these types of proceedings. "That is just as well." said Inspector Foxglove. "This will be quite a unique investigation from the start."

Well, now the young man has left Westwich and our story- but not in the manner we presumed. Still, we were right. He returned to London. We said he would. Let the reader no longer doubt our word.

***

Not long after, a letter was received by the Mr Pimsleur in their temporary housing. It was addressed to Mr Pimsleur and was, in content, concerned primarily with his daughter, Hildegard. The letter was from a cousin of Mr Pimsleur, making it a letter from Hildegard's second cousin, and it was a letter of offer to come to London and live with the second cousin, her husband and their three children as a sort of companion and nurse to the children.

This letter had not arrived without notice or without effort on Mr Pimsleur's part. He had, once they began to settle in new lodgings, begun sending queries out to relations far and wide to obtain a situation for his elder daughter. Their circumstances being drastically changed now, it had become necessary to find something for her. There was no Pimsleur income to be relied upon- it had all been invested years ago into the farm- and what little the family had left, would not last long on four family members.

Hildegard, knowing her duty, began packing at once and was done far sooner than she anticipated. She had nearly no earthly belongings and hardly a bag to put them in. Penelope sat by herself in the window until Hildegard joined her. The two sisters, with a lifetime of words shared, now sat silently together, about to be apart for the first time in their short lives.

14A LETTERS BETWEEN CONSPIRATORS

The following brief missives were sent to (and then from) London by special arrangement and written in code:

C,

the town meeting went as well or better than expected. I am happy to report that the entire public opinion of the people of W and surrounding neighbourhood is firmly against you and they are now perfectly convinced you are, in fact, the notorious OB! I confess, I did not think it would be so easy to convince them you had fooled them, but clearly, they hold your abilities in high regard.

Although I realise this inconveniences you mightily, I undertake to remind you this is a necessary and strategic move on our part as we track down and apprehend the real OB.

As we discussed, you will stay put in London for the time being and I will keep you updated on the course of my investigation here.

Yours in Justice,
F

***

F,

It was with mixed feeling I received your letter. Although I hold to the greater mission of the capture and prosecution of OB, I own my misgivings as to the deliberate tarnishment of my name and reputation in the neighbourhood of W.

However, I remain resolute and determined to see this through to the end. No fear!

Yours in Temporary Disgrace,
C

***

C,

Remain in place, in the strength of justice, knowing your perseverance will result in the apprehension of the true criminal and the end of his reign of terror.

Stalwart and Resolute,
F

***

F,

I thank you for your words of encouragement. I apologize for my delayed response. It has become necessary to be less frequent to the post office in order to not be so regular in my habits in case someone has their eye on me.

With Great Trepidation yet Greater Trust,
C

14B LETTERS BETWEEN SISTERS

Now a series of letters began blazing a distinct trail between London and Westwich, with each of the Pimsleur sisters' respective address across the front.

"My Dearest Penelope…" one began.

"My Even-Dearer Hildegard…" began the reply.

One letter ended, "with all the love of a heart half-left behind, Pen."

Another ended as, "with love greater than all the distances, Hilde."

And so forth.

For our purposes, it is not necessary to include these letters or submit any included details for your perusal; excepting certain items which will serve the story we are telling now. Some of these letters contain opinions which might be useful to the reader in ascertaining the sisters' (and in particular, Penelope's) frame of mind concerning Mr Caleb Cheswick. There are a number of references to his personage scattered throughout their early correspondence, but he is never directly named.

For example, Hildegard wrote this in one of her letters;

"It is with great pleasure, my dearest sister, that I report I have not seen that villain and tormenter of our family since my arrival in London. It is my worst fear and I cannot be rid of it. Despite the enormity of this city, with all its streets and alleys, I fear seeing him in the street. I cannot think what I might do, or say and at the same time I wonder, I wonder if I would say anything- indeed, could I say anything or would I be rooted to the sidewalk (or floorboards) in terror? Could I summon the courage to speak or move and would I want to even if I could?"

Another time, Penelope had this to say in the midst of a paragraph on baking;

"...but I certainly hope that certain person stays well away from you, or I will find a bread pan large enough to end his misery!"

This was a shocking thing for Penelope to write, or even consider, and this imagery communicated strongly to Hildegard her sister's state of mind. Needless to say, Foxglove's plan had taken full effect in the minds of even the Pimsleurs and, for that, was to be commended in his efficacy as a master planner. In later letters, this reference to baking a bread pan with Mr Cheswick in it would appear more like a humble remonstrance in comparison to the vividly described punishments the sisters (in particular, Penelope) imaginatively dealt out in their letters to one another. Only once did Hildegard feel the need to caution Penelope about the state of her soul, which led to a heart-felt repentance and a slight reduction of vitriol.

14C FATHER LEAMAS' SERMON

On Sunday morning, Father Leamas had begun with a short reading:

"Ps 27 'For by Your Light do we see light.'

I have chosen these words with design, if possible, to disturb some part in this audience of half an hour's sleep, for the convenience of transmitting to you some manner of understanding regarding common, or ordinary, light, the source of common, or ordinary, light and Light Himself, whereof we are all second-born brothers.

There is one mortal disadvantage to which all preaching, and indeed if I am permitted to observe, all of life is subject, that those who, by their own wickedness, or their own laziness, or spleen, or hatred toward religion, stand in greatest need of correction and because of which will lead us to employ our minds rather any way other than regarding or attending to the business before us.

It is, namely blindness, this moral disadvantage I refer to. It may also be referred to in truth as sickness or malady, or even the tragic spiral toward which disinterest is ultimately the only end. I have determined today to share with you these few brief thoughts and elevate them beyond mere contemplation of the common and ordinary and elevate our minds to a place of great understanding.

First, I shall produce the account of Creation for an understanding of the solution, before addressing the problem.

Secondly, I shall summon the the words of the Psalmist and St Paul to aid us.

Thirdly, I shall get forth the the Personage of Christ.

Lastly, I shall offer a remedy- indeed, the only remedy- against the great and spreading darkness of our days.

Firstly, Moses faithfully records for us the account of Creation, transported as he was to the beginning of time to witness and bear witness to the extraordinary darkness into which God spoke, and thereby by bring forth revelation of the exact moment in which Light appeared to illuminate all. These are his words in first-hand account:

'And God Said, "Let there be Light." and there was Light.'

Father Leamas' Sermon

Consider Moses now, standing in the darkness, his eyes useless, when suddenly comes a voice, strong as wool and soft as thunder, and into the darkness springs Light standing before him. Did I say Light appeared and stood before Moses- I certainly did. Who is Light? Why is He the Firstborn of all Creation? We must examine what we mean when we say Light- but first, let us discern what we mean by Firstborn.

Secondly, St. Paul refers to this in his letter to the believers abroad. He says, plainly, Jesus Christ is the Firstborn. But we know the Son of God is eternal, having existed before the creation- in fact, having always existed with God and as God. There is no knife sharp enough to cut this truth. In this, we gain an understanding, dim though it may be, of the strictness of language and the pitfalls into which it can lead us.

To whit, if young Ms Williams came first into the chapel this morning, we might rightly call her 'First'. By this, however, we do not mean she was first to exist in this universe or that she did not exist before entering the chapel. She existed elsewhere and then she entered the chapel; First. By saying, in that instance, she is 'First', we merely mean she was the first on the scene. I hope that is sufficient.

Let us return to Moses at the dawn of time, as Light appears. A curious thing happens which Moses does not take the time to explain- surely he could hardly keep up with all that was happening around him! Moses tells us plainly that In the Beginning, Light appeared. But then, by strange use of language, tells us that on Day Four of Creation, God created the Sun and Stars- by which we receive light.

Now, let us pause and consider. What wisdom is in these words? Light appeared before the Sun and Stars. What is the source of light, then? Well, we must consider this. And we must draw a distinction between what we mean by common light and Light. The words of the Psalmist help us discern the difference: "By Your Light do we see light.".

Thirdly, there is a difference between Light and common light. Light is plainly the Christ Himself; the Apostle John, the Beloved, makes this clear. Jesus, as St Paul said, was the Firstborn of all creation- thus, He is the Light from the Beginning. When God said, "let there be Light", Jesus Himself took His cue to appear, first on the scene of creation. All of scripture must be understood in light of the moment Light Himself appeared on the scene as the Firstborn, the Primary, the Focal Point, and indeed all of life must be viewed- not by the light of the Sun and Stars of our intellect or affection but- by the Light Who is the Son of God. Without this understanding, we will be doomed to live in infinite darkness.

Lastly, now that we understand this, we may turn our attention briefly to a statement which Jesus makes, that is, a truth which He sheds His own Light on, that we might better discern and know the truth. He turns and addresses His disciples in this manner,

'You are the Light of the world.' This is a truth incomprehensible without wisdom and the very Spirit of God to help us understand. He certainly does not mean, by this proclamation, that his disciples are now the Sun and the Stars. No. He is, in some way, bequeathing to them the title of Light, which He Himself had carried since the beginning of Creation.

It is only in the Light of Who He Is that we can discern who we ourselves truly are and only in that Light, then, can we understand and appreciate the truth of who our brothers are. Where we fail, where we stumble in the darkness, is outside the Light of Who He Is allowed in our life. Thus, our sin against our brother can only be committed in darkness- not in the darkness which is only the absence of the Sun or Stars, but the darkness which is the absence of Him as Light and the subsequent absence of understanding ourselves as Light, if we also be disciples.

I am reminded of the man born blind, who, by by a certain miracle of medicine could suddenly see. He spoke to his wife, saying, 'All my life I have heard of Light. Now that I can see it for myself, tell me what it is?'

He pointed to the Sun, saying, 'Is that Light?'

'No, that is a source of light.' she replied.

He pointed to the lamp on the table, saying, 'Is that Light?'

'No, that is a source of light.' she replied.

He pointed to the stars at night, saying, 'Is that Light?'

'No, that is a source of light.' she replied.

He despaired of ever seeing Light until one day he met a Painter, who painted a fog in a gorge at sunrise.

The man born blind asked the painter, 'What are you painting?'

'Light!' the Painter shouted and pointed to the fog in the gorge, 'There is Light for you!'

And the man born blind rushed headlong into the gorge, desperate for Light, and plunged to his death before the Painter could stop him.

That which we see plainly with our eyes cannot be perceived without Light. Surely, brethren, these things ought not so to be.

"He that hath ears to hear let him hear."

And God give us all, grace to hear and receive His Holy Word to the salvation of our own souls."

This sermon, delivered by Father Leamas, and any good it might have done, was entirely negated by the town's fixation on the final story regarding The Man Born Blind. The story was considered a shocking and unnecessarily discomfiting addition to an otherwise acceptable homily. It was talked about for upwards of three days in some parts of the neighborhood and then, like every other sermon in Father Leamas' career, it was summarily dismissed

Father Leamas' Sermon

with words similar to "A nice sermon, although I wish he would talk more about St Stephen and his transfixation. I like that story better."

15 INSPECTOR FOXGLOVE, *CONSTABULE PRO TEMPORE*

Let us now return to Mr Caleb Cheswick, one-time *Constabule Pro Tempore* of Westwich (and surrounding neighbourhood), but now a supposed fugitive and purported desperate criminal on the run from the law. According to Inspector Foxglove- and, no one in Westwich had any second thoughts regarding the veracity of his accusation or even contemplated doubting his word on the matter- Caleb Cheswick had instigated the series of burglaries and had ignited the devastating fire at the Pimsleur Estate. There was no handed-down story in the entire history of Westwich full of so much betrayal and destruction as the one Foxglove had told the town that night at the meeting.

This was good for the plan Foxglove had concocted. The success of it depended on everyone in the neighborhood believing the story implicating Caleb Cheswick. The afternoon they met near the North Bridge, Foxglove had outlined for the young man his plan to publicly pronounce ("pin it on" were the words he had used) Cheswick as the burglar and arsonist in the hopes of throwing the real villain off the trail of the true investigation. They had agreed that London was the best place for Cheswick to hide in the meantime and he had gone forthwith, with two leather overnight bags and a hat and coat. He had walked down to Brakton in the gathering dusk and hired a local cab from there to the train station, and thence to London with no adventure.

Immediately upon leaving the train station in London, he sent word to Foxglove of his arrival and then, two leather bags in hand, he began to walk in the city. A passerby would have taken no notice, and hardly anyone did. He was one of a thousand visitors to that enormous city and he, for all intents and purposes, disappeared into the mass of locals and visitors as one of them. But the route he took truly was one of a desperate criminal- he walked in one direction, then turned, then turned again. Sometimes he would enter a shop, only to exit again and walk the opposite of the the direction he had come by.

He took so much time, and by so many intricate ways, double-backs, alleys, shops and even a loop around Trafalgar which sent him right on in the same direction as before; he thought even Foxglove would be impressed by his craftiness. In the end, though, he simply hopped into a local cab and gave the driver an address well-known to the cabman. And that was how Caleb Cheswick went into hiding in London.

Foxglove had suggested a certain part of London and a certain street which Cheswick might spend an extended time in absentia without anyone asking too many questions or too many eyes watching and Cheswick indeed found lodgings where all these items were checked off the list, as it were. Once again, Cheswick privately felt that, had Foxglove known or seen his precise lodging of choice, the fabled Inspector would have acknowledged Cheswick as possessing a surprising instinct for subterfuge.

The room itself was just that- a room. Small and dark. In it, he found a simple bed, a wash basin, a table upon which the basin sat- these made a precarious pair- and a frame hung on the wall. The rug was in its last stages of staying raveled. The ceiling might have once had an access to the attic or potato storage, but it was nailed shut now. There was a door (thank goodness for that) and a window through which only the tiniest burglar might gain entry. This was Caleb Cheswick's base of operations for the foreseeable future.

Whatever other rooms there may have been in the building, or house, or whatever it was called, Caleb needed only the one. He placed his two leather overnight bags on the foot of the bed. He inspected the bedding- he decided it would do but he would find out about a second table or even a small desk. Something to put a candle on would be a great service as well. Fugitives cannot be choosers, he reminded himself. Gingerly, Cheswick tested the structure of the bed and sat down. This was where he pulled out from his pocket Foxglove's first letter and this is where he wrote his first reply- both of which have been treated in an earlier chapter- on this bed and without a desk.

***

Meanwhile, under the pretense of a 'clean slate', *tabula rasa*, and so forth, Inspector Foxglove now began an aggressive campaign of visiting the scenes of the burglaries once again. What he needed to be sure of most, was there were no lingering clues pointing to Orton Black which Cheswick may have missed in his preliminary and unscientific investigation. He anticipated the victim's patience would be wearing thin, but encouraged them with the knowledge that they would be aiding him in bringing Caleb Cheswick *nom Orton Black* to justice- which, of course, was not the true aim of these investigations.

The town of Westwich and its surrounding neighborhood seemed to be under a revival of lawfulness now that Inspector Foxglove was made the *Constabule Pro Tempore*. The feeling of the people regarding the suitedness of Cheswick to succeed his illustrious father as Constable became more apparent day by day, revealed in small ways, this and that, to be a largely negative one. Add to that, the compounding of their anguish and anger regarding Cheswick's (supposed) betrayal in the robberies and complicated further by the arson- it was a real stew of animosity. Rising out of this discontent, however, was a new (or, as we have said, revived) respect and admiration for the constabulary. Both the office and the man were spoken of in reverent tones and with gracious words. It was a feeling of relief and confidence.

Foxglove had taken up the office of Constable and sat in the chair Cheswick once had. A wash of gratitude made its way to the small office several times a day in the form of baked goods and (purported) special blends of herbal teas and other niceties which the grateful women of Westwich thought proper toward the new champion of the law. The towering figure of justice told each gift-bringer that no royalty had ever been so gladly received and welcomed or so lavishly gifted as he was by their gift (scones, muffins, etc.) which was, of course, entirely untrue. Had it been true, it ought to have caused the townspeople to feel sorry for their monarchs through the ages but instead, the possibility of its truth was registered in their minds as good as a royal stamp of approval on their very ovens.

This became so constant a flow that Foxglove stopped taking breakfast in the tavern in the mornings and simply took a basket (a basket which one humble citizen had left behind, full of braided breads of varying qualities) of fresh baked breakfasts and lunches with him nearly everywhere he went. He could be seen in town, in his office or on his visits carrying a basket under his arm.

As we have said, Foxglove began a new campaign of canvasses and investigations- some of which will be related here- as a way of covering his tracks as he set forth on his real campaign. The first visit he made was to the Blankenship estate and we will follow him there, even as he carefully avoids Father Leamas and his wild theories about the nature of light, colour and reality.

The poor maid who worked for the Blankenships opened the door one morning to find the towering figure in his long black coat and a basket on his elbow.

"Good morning, young lady. I do not have an appointment- I wish to speak with Mr Blankenship on an important matter of justice." Foxglove said, with a bow usually reserved for the masters, not the servants.

Such strength and purpose! Yet a softness belied by the basket and the bow! Such a perfectly brushed black coat! The poor young maid who worked for the Blankenships was instantly under his spell and in the coming days swooned several times over at the memory. Fortunately, in the critical moment, she kept her composure (or, perhaps maintained her fear of the Blankenships) and invited Inspector Foxglove into the house. She took his hat and coat (perfectly brushed!) and sat him in the library, taking him immediately for a man of learning. Then she rushed to tell Mr Blankenship the Inspector was in the sitting room, announced but without an appointment.

Foxglove had no time to settle himself into the chair he had found so comfortable on his last visit as Mr Niles Blankenship came through the wide arched entry of the sitting room.

"I apologise for keeping you waiting, Inspector. No one told me you were here. The wretched help come and go and wander at their own whim- I would release all of them if I thought it would do any good." Niles Blankenship said, the poor young maid standing just behind him. He didn't look at her when he spoke next. "Go tell Miss Blankenship the inspector is here."

Off the girl scurried.

Foxglove, annoyed he had no time to enjoy the chair, waved his hand and rose slowly from his chair.. "If only, Mr Blankenship. If only."

"Please, Inspector. Come with me into my study and we will discuss whatever it is you-" Niles Blankenship began to say- but he was cut off by the entry of his sister.

"I am so sorry, Inspector. No one told me you were here." Ms Blankenship said. She offered her hand as though seeking consolation for their troubles with the help.

Foxglove, ever diplomatic, received her graciously and with a flair which made her forget her troubles for the moment. At Mr Blankenship's lead, they trouped into his study. Seated comfortably, Foxglove took his time explaining his purpose.

"Mr Blankenship." He said. He turned to the sister, "Ms Blankenship."

"Please," she said in as sweet a voice as she could muster, "call me Pruniprismia."

Inspector Foxglove, seated most comfortably, foremost man of the world and armed with rapier intelligence, struggled to understand the name she had named for herself. He had never heard it before and was doubtful he had even heard correctly. He knew she had not said Penelope or Priscilla. She continued her gaze at him. It certainly wasn't Drizella, but he thought he might have misheard the 'P' as a 'D', which led him down the path of Druscilla and Denelopemia or perhaps a modernisation of Deianeira. Never one to panic, he merely returned her sweetened smile and said, "Of course.

"It is necessary, now, to begin to trace back over the investigation which that false constable, Caleb Cheswick, conducted. We must determine, in order to bring him to justice, clues which will also connect him- like links in a chain- to his crimes; and by such a chain of impenetrable clues and facts we will turn the mighty winch of justice and thereby we shall pull him into the full custody of the law. As such, I require full access to the grounds and the house itself. I shall spend most of the day combing it in hopes of discovery." Foxglove said.

"What hopes, Inspector? It has been too long, hasn't it, since the crimes?" Niles Blankenship said.

"The evidences may have faded, sir, but I have not. I am still in full possession of my powers as an investigator. Further, I hold to the hope laid out in scripture- that is, the confident expectation. When I say hope, I do not mean a wishful thinking or a fanciful lark. When I say I hope, I mean I am fully confident. Fully confident." Foxglove said.

That seemed to satisfy both the Blankenship siblings, who knew better than to question an invocation of scripture- especially a scripture they did not recognize.

Foxglove, reluctant to leave his comfortable chair, but wanting to avoid any situation where he might be expected to correctly pronounce Miss Blankenship's name, took up his hat and said he had better begin his formal investigation and would need the room please? The Blankenships retired to give him space.

16 PEN QUITS WESTWICH

"My Dearest Hildegard," Penelope Pimsleur wrote to her sister, "I was at the post office just this morning and the Blankenship siblings, arrived in town for other purposes I imagine, followed me inside and struck up their own conversation, ostensibly standing in line behind me, but surely to torment me.

"Oh, wasn't that party lovely last night?" said Ms Blankenship.

"All the fashionable young men were there, certainly." said Mr Blankenship.

And so on.

But despite their inability to see these were not topics I cared for, they are very adept at recognizing when their methods of getting under someone's skin aren't working. So they tried a different tack.

"Sister, do you remember the Pimsleurs in their glory?" said Mr Blankenship.

"They had a wonderful house, brother." said Ms Blankenship.

"Do you remember I once proposed to Ms Pimsleur?" said Mr Blankenship.

"I do. I certainly do. How the mighty have fallen." said Ms Blankenship. She sadly shook her head.

All this was in my full hearing.

"It pains me. It pains me. That one offer of kindness- a partnership between equals- would have brought the young Ms Pimsleur into our family and made her one of us. Had she only been wise enough to accept, I could- with her as my wife- embrace her whole family as my own and draw them near in their time of need. I would cover them as a hen her chickens." said Mr Blankenship.

"You magnanimity and graciousness would not, in that case, be so restricted as it is now by common sense, by dignity, by decency." said Ms Blankenship.

"But it troubles me to see someone so young, so capable, so full of promise, and yet so foolish. So unconcerned with the plight of her own family." said Mr Blankenship.

"It is a bitter pill to take, is it not? To see those you could help, shun the very hand you extend to them?" said Ms Blankenship.

"Painful indeed." said Mr Blankenship.

Ms Blankenship turned her attention now to me and spoke soothingly to me.

"Penelope, I want you to know I know what you are going through. You and your family are having such a difficult time." Ms Blankenship said, spreading her hands to me.

"You know what I am going through?" I asked. But Ms Blankenship seemed to me to be spreading her hood, like a cobra.

"Oh yes, my brother and I were robbed earlier this year- in the spring. It is a traumatic experience, to be sure." Ms Blankenship said.

"I'm not sure I understand, Ms Blankenship?" I said, quite sure I did perfectly.

"Isn't it obvious, dear? The fire at your home and the theft at our home. It's all too horrifying." Ms Blankenship said.

"We were robbed, as well, Ms Blankenship. I imagine you are comparing those two things- the robberies which were, in fact, quite similar. I cannot imagine you are comparing a theft (which we both did experience) to the fact of our entire estate, our livelihood, my childhood home- burned to the ground?" I said.

"Loss is loss, Penelope. I know just what you are going through." Ms Blankenship said.

I cannot, ever, put into words the fury in my heart toward them and my mind spun with a thousand things to say- and even more to do!

I shall write you a decent letter in a day or two. Until then, this will have to suffice.

In Despair,
Your Sister

***

"Dearest Heart of My Own Heart,

I raged when I read your letter and wept when I finished. We are not well, you and I.

The worst thing which could happen to me here has happened! While you have come under weapons of assailment, I have seen with my own eyes the villain of our nightmares! He whom we do not speak of! The perpetrator of all our troubles! The arsonist and thief of our home! Caleb Cheswick is in London! You must alert Inspector Foxglove, tell him to mobilise- whatever he mobilises! This is an opportunity which must not be overlooked.

I will tell you what happened. I was walking the children (you remember, Mildred and Manfred, the twins). We were in the park, they in their perambulator and I, sitting on the park bench. It was a perfectly lovely day full of sunshine- which moments are so rare here in London, let alone whole days such as that! How little did I know the darkness which would settle on my soul!

Anyway, we were sitting in the park for a long time- I even had time to read a little. You know how difficult it has been for me to find time to read here, with the twins and worrying about Mother and Father and keeping up with you. But I have found a perfectly delightful little book about people who have nothing bad in their lives and they only go from pleasant day to pleasant day with nothing but the slightest of inconveniences- inconveniences which, of course, set them off in spirals of despair- and I sometimes feel like shouting at them that I have seen far worse in a single day than they have in their entire pleasant lives! And sometimes I remember how nice is it to be overwrought about small and inconsequential things and it endears me to the characters all the more.

I had got quite a lot of reading done and was beginning to think I might need to move to a shady spot for my complexion (which threatens at all moments to go a hideous color), so I did. And I read a little more. And all this time, the twins hardly stirred- as if they knew the reading I craved and deigned to gift it to me.

Anyway, as I was saying, I was reading. Well, I finished the book! I cannot tell you how long it has been (3 months) since I finished a whole book and it was really a lovely book. I will give you a recommendation. The story is about two friends who have been friends for ever so long and they got into adventures as small children (not real adventures, of course, but climbing trees together and getting stung by bees and that sort of thing) but now they are grown and there are no more adventures and they sometimes each of them crave adventures again. Of course, neither tells the other about this secret wish for adventure and their lives are perfectly normal and carefree right up until... the end, when they realise and discover the greatest adventure is a treasured friend with whom who can share tea.

It was perfectly lovely to not have anything terrible happen. Do you remember the Icy Blue Hand of Death? I read that over and over until the cover fell off and I kept reading it, pinching the pages together. Until our own tragedy, Pen, I craved such awfulness and adventure. Now, I just want to sit on the veranda and have our own tea again.

Oh. I saw Caleb Cheswick as I walked the twins home.
Tell Foxglove!
This; our most desperate hour! He; our only hope!

Yours for Tea, Hildegard

***

It is now my duty to give a report updating the reader on Mr Caleb Cheswick, his activities, his comings and goings and to provide an example of his behavior so the reader will not be caught unawares in future chapters. Since Hildegard saw him in London, we must suppose he has not left our story quite yet. Or, why else would he appear again?

These details of Cheswick were provided by certain associates of Inspector Foxglove; individuals with extended connections to Scotland Yard and familiar with Foxglove's ways and means. It should be said these individuals he recruited to keep an eye on Mr Cheswick for his own safety, and not because he harbored any suspicion toward Mr Cheswick in any way. The news he received and which I relay to you was as surprising and shocking to him as it will be to you.

Reports began coming from London every few days from local contacts to the effect that Mr Caleb Cheswick was generally keeping to the suggested schedules given him by Inspector Foxglove, with certain small deviations. These deviations in schedule seemed to grow over time until one day he was not to be found on the streets at all.

Further, certain unknown individuals began visiting his rooms at odd hours. One, a man with a pronounced limp very early in the morning. Two, a man with a cruel scar was seen leaving- though never having entered by the front door- in the middle of the night.

These two characters of dubious character greatly concerned Foxglove back in Westwich, when he heard of them. He made orders for a doubled watch and greater caution. Foxglove knew perfectly well Cheswick could not have been the criminal Orton Black, but what if there were s second criminal? What if someone had gotten to Cheswick and turned his mind against Foxglove? This question began to gnaw on the edges of Foxglove's mind.

Things seemed to quiet down almost immediately in London. Suddenly, Mr Cheswick was back on the prescribed routine, there were no midnight visitors, and things were going according to plan again.

***

Penelope wondered what this day would be like; the day she heard Caleb Cheswick had been sighted. It had been inevitable. She knew it would come but knew she could not prepare herself for it. She let it hit her and felt the impact. He would have to answer for his betrayal of her and her family.

What the police did- did not matter to her.

What Foxglove did- did not matter to her.

What the courts tried, decided, or carried out- did not matter to her.

What mattered to Penelope Pimsleur was not the hot pursuit of the guilty criminal or the cold process of justice. There was no thrill of chase. There was no solace in passed time. There was only him- face to face with her- saying he had done what he had done. What she did to him, or did not do, was entirely unknown. She only knew she must have that one moment with him. This was her crusade, to watch him speak the words of confession. She made a visit to Father Leamas, to gain his counsel in her state of mind.

"Crusades, don't always turn out the way one plans." Father Leamas had said. "Centuries ago, the People's Crusade, considered a noble and just cause, and led by some distant past relatives of most everyone here in Westwich, culminated in 1096 at the Battle of Civetot (in then-present Turkey) where, coincidentally, two Turkish spies were responsible for spreading a rumor that the Germans had meanwhile taken both Xerigordon and Nicaea to the effect that the desire for easy plundering ultimately motivated the entire army to strike out for Nicaea. Along the road, they were ambushed by the Turkish army in a narrow place and were quite devastated by the ambush (it had been Turkish spies who spread the rumor to start with, after all), not to mention the thousands of arrows which the Turks rained down on them.

"In 1097, Crusaders left Constantinople and made the two week trek to Nicaea (which hadn't been taken by the Germans after all, only the surrounding countryside had been looted) to exact their revenge. Godfrey of Bouillon and Bohemond of Taranto were the first to arrive with their contingents. They began building their engines and laid the siege as others arrived. Sultan Kilij Arslan I, being away fighting elsewhere, returned to defend his people when the city begged him to. Meanwhile Emperor Alexios I, camped back at Pelecanum, sent Manuel Boutoumites with 2,000 soldiers to the front of the siege, ostensibly to fortify the siege but secretly to negotiate the surrender of the city without the rest of the Crusaders' knowledge. Plundering, of course, being unsporting in the event of a formal surrender, would leave the Crusaders sour. Boutoumites and Arslan had negotiated the surrender in secret and deprived the Crusaders of their well-earned loot. In retrospect, the Crusaders wished they hadn't told the Emperor about their progress until they had gotten their looting in, but it couldn't be helped- it had been a siege, after all!"

Penelope Pimsleur, for her part, was determined not to be undermined in her own crusade to London to confront Caleb Cheswick (perhaps she was not intentionally referencing this particular historical moment at Nicaea). Though Hildegard had begged her to go straight to Inspector Foxglove with the whereabouts of Mr Cheswick, Penelope decided that the interference of that champion of the law would be unwelcome and keep her from her purpose. Instead of divulging the information that Caleb Cheswick could be found in London (which Foxglove, of course, unbeknownst to Penelope, already knew perfectly) Penelope kept the information to herself and let it burn in her heart. What Foxglove would have told her had she gone to him, is very hard to say.

Penelope's train ride to London was swift and uneventful. Her sister and uncle were there to greet her and their meeting on the platform was as it should have been between sisters of such a bond as they had.

Their uncle and aunt were unaware of the real reason for Penelope's visit, and assumed she was only in the city to visit her sister and see the sights as any tourist would. They made arrangements to give Hildegard a day or two off to accommodate this and Penelope graciously thanked them for their exceptional courtesy. Thus, Penelope and Hildegard Pimsleur spent two days alone, only returning each evening just before dinner.

Their time was not really spent doing anything other than sitting in public places and talking together while they watched the crowds for the familiar face of Caleb Cheswick. It was Penelope's full intention- and singular hope- she might see Mr Cheswick and confront him in broad daylight in front of every stranger in London, especially if it could be done in front of a famous landmark.

Hildegard, in their first such watchful sitting expressed her concern about Penelope's decision to not inform Inspector Foxglove and allow he and the other police to apprehend the criminal and bring him to justice. Penelope firmly explained justice was not her intention- only the confession was important to her.

"He did this atrocious thing and left without allowing me to chastise him for it, Hilde. That is why I am here." Penelope said.

17 THE DEVIL'S ELBOW

In Which Mr Rampert, Master of Huffington-In-Box, tells an enlightening and bizarre story about his past and we begin to realise it has something to do with our particular story.

"Have you ever heard of the Devil's Elbow, Inspector?" Mr Rampert said. He had leaned in close, spoke in half whispers and seemed to have once again been miraculously cured of his cough.

"The devil's elbow inspector?" Foxglove repeated skeptically. "No. I don't think I'm familiar with-"

Rampert had cut him off.

"No, The Devil's Elbow! Have you ever heard of The Devil's Elbow?" Rampert said.

"I've never concerned myself with the anatomy of that-" Foxglove had begun again and Rampert cut him off again.

The Devil's Elbow

"NO! No, Sir! The Devil's Elbow is a place!" Rampert said. He appeared to consider and started again. "Let me start another way. If you don't know the place called The Devil's Elbow, then I better start from the beginning. You had better get comfortable. Would you like a smoke?"

Foglove shook his head.

Mr Rampert took a deep breath and gathered his thoughts. He studiously lit an enormous cigar and exhaled several large puffs of smoke before he began. It was clear to Foxglove the man was about to unburden himself in some way. Something like the old conflict of the criminal- so familiar now to Foxglove- displayed itself in the old man's features; all at once, the relief of telling his story and the fear someone would hear.

"I had just been made 2nd Lieutenant, Third Company of the 46th Brigade, Expeditionary Force for the 9th Regiment. I was still green in her his majesty's service. I had been made an officer because of my father's influence with the regimental commander, Colonel Paxson. I had been born a twin but no one knew which of us was the eldest so in order to sort out the problem of inheritance, my father sent me and my twin brother off to the war with the invocation that whoever returned alive would inherit his sizable estate.

"I didn't know anything about a map and when they asked me which way was north I asked, in return, which country I was in- thinking it would have a bearing on my bearing, if you take my meaning- the country I was in turned out to be India, by the way. We were stationed in Mafeking- a critical asset but an entirely unsuitable place for gentlemen to gather for any reason other than to drink and fight. But there I was, an officer and a cartographer to boot, and learned pretty quickly which way was up. My commanding officer, Major Perdue, saw to that."

Foxglove interrupted.

"Major Perdue?! Not William Perdue, surely? I knew a Perdue sent to Mafeking. A surly rascal from Devonshire with a long brown mustache?!" he said. Rampert nodded.

"The very same. He was a strict commander; and a principled gentleman." Rampert said.

"Cannot be the same, then, Mr Rampert. Excuse my outburst of enthusiasm. The Will Perdue I knew was a rascal, prone to opium and fond of brown girls. He volunteered for the army just to be near his vices- and he considered the carrying of a firearm to be a fringe benefit. I can't imagine such a man being promoted through the ranks." Foxglove said.

Rampert nodded his head emphatically.

"The very same, Inspector, the very same man. He had his vices like any man, but he was a highly principled gentleman." Rampert said.

Foxglove began to protest, but it was Rampert's turn to interrupt him.

"Favored his left leg and had a scar about here, didn't he, Will Perdue from Devonshire?" Rampert said.

Foxglove nodded, astounded.

"Maybe you don't agree with his principles, Inspector. But the man lived them thoroughly. So, as I was saying, Major Perdue set me straight and gave me my first lessons in cartography. In the first year I was there, I took part in three sorties, two outbreaks of malaria, and five true expeditionary assignments. By the end of that first year, I had a pretty good idea that I would never leave India alive and began making arrangements to that end.

"Several months into my second year in India, still out of Mafeking, we had cut our way through the jungle to the northwest for weeks when we were ambushed yet again by the enemy (though God knows it was their jungle before we got there) and in the confusion of battle, not to mention our complete lack of ammunition, we were routed and it was suddenly every man for himself.

"Deep in the jungle, with only my pack on my back, I hid from the fight (couldn't very well fight bullets and knives with my maps) and by nightfall I was alone in the jungle and my Company was lost. In the morning I began navigating my way back with a damaged compass and a machete I had pulled from the death grip of one of my men. I was two days on my own when I heard them. I won't frighten you with ghosts; it was the other two survivors of my Company. They had tracked me and shown themselves when they were certain it was me. The three of us shook hands and cried manful tears in the Indian jungle."

Foxglove listened with increasing interest.

"We never stayed in one place too long- a few hours at most- and kept moving as fast as our supplies and exhaustion would allow, until we came quite suddenly on a village not on our maps at all. It was a small and backward community, due to its remote location on the river- and that's when we discovered how far off course we were. The river we had been following was not what we thought it was- we had been hiking for four days up a tributary of the river we ought to have been following.

"The locals actually helped us realise where we were and were entirely hospitable. They didn't seem to care whose side we were on as they were far too remote to be on anyone's side to begin with. We spent two nights there, taking turns keeping watch, whatever they said about safety and hospitality. The second night, they told us about the Devil's Elbow, and warned us not to go any further up the tributary. Which, of course, we had no intention of now we knew we were going the wrong way to begin with.

"The Devil's Elbow is what they called it but I can assure you, young man, though it may not translate into our tongue well, in the local vernacular it is a terrifying name. The tributary we had been following led into a gorge, they told us, where it became very steep on both sides and dangerous with rocky outcroppings like teeth in a crocodile's mouth- this gorge or ravine then takes a sharp, very sharp, degree of turn- and that is The Devil's Elbow.

"Having had shelter and food for two days, though, this notion of the Devil's Elbow fascinated us and the three of us decided to take a hike and have a look for ourselves.

"What we found was exactly what the villagers had told us about. The jungle was thick at that point- double and even triple canopy. The village itself was the only relief of sun for miles around. Anyway, The Devil's Elbow was everything they described to us and more. We stood near the top of the gorge, then lay on our bellies and crawled to the edge, to look down into the abyss of foaming water, razored rocks and sheer walls of slickest stone, at least twenty meters below. A man who went down there would never make it out alive, Inspector.

"We lay there, like boys, mesmerised by the sight until we shook ourselves and decided we better get back. So we started to, but then my eye caught a flash of color in the rapids below. I assumed it was a rainbow- a tiny and perfectly natural sign of peace in the midst of the chaos below. The juxtaposition transfixed me. And then I realised it wasn't a rainbow- but something else."

"What was it, Mr Rampert?" Foxglove asked.

"Treasure, Inspector. Actual, real, treasure." Rampert said.

Foxglove's eyebrows inquired on this point of grammar. Rampert raised his right hand in protest.

"We didn't know it at that very moment, but we knew something was down there and that something was worth finding out. We knew, deep in our bones, there was something down there. And we knew we had to take it for ourselves. We made a pact, then and there, on the edge of the gorge, that we would return to that place and bring all the equipment necessary to retrieve it.

"The three of us returned to the village, and several grueling weeks later, we were back in Mafeking where we learned (though we had suspected) we were the only survivors of the Third Company- no one else had returned. And, in fact, we had been presumed dead along with the rest, it had been so long with no word. We were all awarded medals and given promotions for the brave heroics of not dying. The Third Company was reconstituted and I was given a new command. As Third Company, then, we began mission assignments in road making- a road which our commanding officers believed to be heading along the river. I suppose, it was along the river, but I and my two friends knew it was also on the way to the treasure we had found.

"For a year we built that road and then, once it was well cut through the jungle and developed well past the tributary which led to our treasure. Well, we all three subsequently resigned our commissions and began a trading company; a Limited which would allow us to use the road as a trade route, ostensibly, but in reality we were preparing our way to the treasure.

"We had a small trade profit amidst all the competition but our goal was not the trade route. Little by little we began moving supplies and machinery- often by night- up the tributary to the little village. I will not tire you with the details of that year, the squabbles with the villagers, the difficulties with the army, the terrible logistical burden of what all we were trying to accomplish. Suffice to say, more than a year after that, we had loaded the treasure onto our own ocean vessel and were headed out of India. We traveled the entire continent west of there, stopping where we could and selling the treasure off, piece by piece, for currency, which we would then exchange later for other currencies. We did this along the entire coast and around the horn of Africa. We were not sailors, but we had hired a small crew and we stayed close to land, so that when foul weather came up, we could shelter quickly. Our cargo was far too valuable to be lost at sea.

"Business was not good for most of the African portion, but then we turned east into the Mediterranean, and that was a very, very good summer. Port to port, selling off our treasures and gradually exchanging our currencies until we made port in Malaga. By then, we had sold off everything we had found in the Devil's Elbow and were carrying nothing but British pounds. At Malaga, we went our separate ways, though we all intended to eventually come back to England. And I did. I never saw the other two again."

Rampert leaned forward and stumped out his cigar in the tray, while Foxglove leaned back and absorbed the strange tale. He finally found his voice.

"Mr Rampert, I cannot speak to the legality of your actions- though in that strange land they may have been perfectly legal. As it is quite out of my jurisdiction, I give you my solemn word- I will not breathe a word of this to any living soul." Foxglove said.

"Do I have your word on that, Inspector?" Rampert said.

"Yes. My word, Mr Rampert." Foxglove said.

Rampert smiled.

"Thank you. That is very kind. And quite unnecessary. Even if you did tell someone, the fortune still left to me is entirely safe. No one could ever find it."

"Are you saying, in your long life, you haven't spent it all?" Foxglove said.

"My dear Inspector. I couldn't spend all that fortune in a dozen lifetimes." Mr Rampert said.

"Who else knows about this, Mr Rampert?" Foxglove said.

"No one, of course." Mr Rampert said.

"What about the sailing crew you hired? Did you pay them off?" Foxglove said. "Sailors can be desperate and capable men, why don't you fear them?"

"Oh, perhaps I didn't mention that, Inspector. By the time we reached Madagascar, the three of us had quite thoroughly learned how to sail the boat ourselves- and we left them in Madagascar. They didn't expect that!" Mr Rampert said. "But that was the other side of the world, Inspector. There is nothing to fear from them!"

"Still, Mr Rampert, loose ends and all that." Foxglove warned.

"Your concern is entirely unwarranted." Mr Rampert said.

"Is it? Mr Rampert are you in contact with the other two of your conspirators?" Foxglove said.

"No. We've never had contact since Malaga." Mr Rampert said.

"Mr Rampert, it is my duty, then. I must to raise a concern. A very important concern. Your's is an unusual story and an enormous amount of money, to be direct in my speech." Foxglove said. "In my profession, I hear things. The worlds of crime and crime-fighting intertwine regularly and they share the same stories. And I have, in the past two years, heard two other stories similar to your's. However, the other two stories end in tragedy."

"Go on." Mr Rampert said.

"You never told me the names of the other two men with whom you discovered the treasure of The Devil's Elbow. Allow me to guess at them now." Foxglove said.

"Go on." Mr Rampert said.

"Two years ago, in Germany, a Baron Von Vostbader was found murdered in his home, hung from the balustrade of the main stair in his palatial estate near the Black Forest. His clothes were- well, never mind. His fortune, reputed to be incalculable and kept in a vault in the basement, was never recovered by the police. The vault door had been nearly disintegrated by some fantastic means. But in the ensuing investigation they- the police- did discover his name was not Von Vostbader, and that he was not even German. He was an Englishman, living under a false name. His birth name was Francis Bixby, formerly of the Third Company of the 46th Brigade, Expeditionary Force for the 9th Regiment, Mafeking, Retired."

At the name of his former compatriot, Mr Rampert's face went perfectly pale.

Foxglove continued.

"Next guess. About this time last year, in the south of Spain, a Frenchman by the name of Pierre Gavant was found, also in his home, brutally murdered. The crime scene was so horrific that the government of Spain hushed it up, appalled that such a thing could have happened within its borders. Remember, this is the same region of that same country in which the Christians and Moslems traded atrocities as if they were trading trinkets, and if you need to be reminded, the Spanish Inquisition was, afterall, in Spain.

"Regarding the murdered man, Pierre Gavant was not his real name and he, of course, was not a Frenchman. His name was-"

"Peter Gallant..." Mr Rampert breathed.

"Quite so." Foxglove said. "Peter Gallant, assigned to the Third Company of the 46th Brigade, Expeditionary Force for the 9th Regiment, Mafeking, Retired. Mr Rampert, I believe you are in great danger. Your friends, or conspirators, are dead. Very dead, and their fortunes taken away. And they went to some effort to change their names and conceal their past- and you are still Thomas Rampert!"

Mr Rampert was silent. Stunned by the news, the implications of these revelations still slowly working their way in his mind.

"Mr Rampert, I must continue. Both of these crimes are, as yet, unsolved, but both crimes- both grisly murders- are believed to be the work of Orton Black. Up until this crucial moment, I have been searching for some reason why Orton Black would target this small village of Westwich, a neighborhood of no real consequence." Foxglove looked directly at Mr Rampert. "But Mr Rampert, I believe, no, I am afraid, you are the answer I have been looking for. Orton Black is in Westwich, he is looking for your fortune, and he will stop at nothing, no human decency will dissuade him, from finding it!"

18 INTERVIEW WITH FATHER LEAMAS

In Which Inspector Foxglove Learns Things, But None of the Things Father Leamas Intends for Him to Learn.

"The young people are beating a path to London these days." said Father Leamas. "I heard young Penelope Pimsleur has left Westwich. It just goes to show that two people- let alone three- can look at the very same thing and see two different things. Different, mind you."

> He would have continued but Inspector Foxglove interrupted

him.

"I beg your pardon, Father. Did you say Penelope Pimsleur has left Westwich?" said Foxglove. This troubled him. He had sent Caleb Cheswick to London, of course, but then the elder Pimsleur sister, Hildegard, left for London. Not much he could do about that. Now, with another young person leaving, it was beginning to unsettle him. There was too much movement for such a little town. He liked to have more control over the comings and goings of people of all ages during an investigation of this nature. Where on earth had Penelope Pimsleur gone?

"That's right, Inspector. I heard she left just a few days ago. As I was saying, it shows just how differently two people can look at the same situation." said Father Leamas.

"I beg your pardon, Father. Where did Penelope Pimsleur go?" said Foxglove.

"London." Father Leamas said. "If you and I, for example, both looked at the same book (in this case, let us say the Study on Hominids there) on the same table; we would see two different books. It is the nature of light to always shine the same, but because of how the human eye has evolved over the millenia, you and see the same color in the same light in two different shades."

"I beg your pardon, Father. Did you say Penelope Pimsleur has gone to London? Surely it is only temporary? said Foxglove. These London-bound sisters could expose Foxglove's plan! It was important that neither of them spot Cheswick while he was hiding out in London. Foxglove silently hoped Penelope Pimsleur was only going for a short visit to her sister.

"Yes, to London. But no, not temporary as I had heard. She has gone to earn her way in the larger world. I hear what I hear- there are no two ways of

Interview with Father Leamas

hearing a thing, Inspector." said Father Leamas. "This empirical understanding of light explains perfectly why I may like a certain shade of green silk tie while you, seeing the very same green silk tie in the very same light will be disinclined to like the very, same, green, silk tie! You doubt this? When you find someone who shares your opinion on a green silk tie- whether you and they like it or do not like it- you feel an instant affinity with them and for them. You have found a common bond- you have found someone whose eye has evolved along the same lines as your own! That is a very special and remarkable observation to share. Of course, they may like what you do not see. What I mean is, you and that person may like the same green silk tie- however! You may be seeing one shade and they may be seeing an entirely different shade, but your individual tastes may coincide on the same object even though you are seeing two different colors." Father Leamas leaned back in his chair. He shook his head in amazement. "The evolution of the human eye, Inspector. The evolution of the human eye! What was it the good Baron wrote? 'We are not now what we once were?' He meant it derogatorily, of course, but he wasn't wrong. 'We are not now what we once were'- we are better and more!

"Quite permanent." said Inspector Foxglove. He was thinking of Penelope Pimsleur.

"No. Oh certainly not!" said Father Leamas. He was thinking of the evolution of the human eye.

"NO! Progress does not stop or slow down. It only appears that way because of our place in time; we cannot quickly move to the future or the past as we would like to compare, in real time as it were. No, my good inspector, that is where you are wrong. Allow history to mentor you! Look back at the facts of what the human eye could conceive three thousand years ago and compare it to now, you will see plainly that it is not permanent at all. Only change- progressive change- is permanent. Imagine, Inspector, if you will, what the full evolution- what we christians call redemption- of the human eye will look like. What splendid colours! What depth! What meaning! What distance! What light and bright light! Imagine you had an eagle's eye! Splendid! Quite splendid!"

"You do not think the Pimsleur girl's move to London is permanent, Father?" said Inspector Foxglove.

"It's not a move at all, Inspector- not to my knowledge. It is a visit only." said Father Leamas.

"Only a visit?" said Inspector Foxglove.

"Inspector, I have no idea. I merely heard in town that Penelope Pimsleur had gone to London to see her sister." Leamas shrugged. "That does not sound permanent to me. It sounds, in fact, very temporary and I'm not sure what difference it makes either way? Unless you are concerned with the population figures and migratory trends of Westwich and its surrounding neighborhood?" said Father Leamas.

Interview with Father Leamas

"No, I suppose not, Father." said Inspector Foxglove. "But as you said, the young people do seem to be beating a path to London these days. Do you think it is a moral issue?"

"No, not at all, Inspector. A moral issue? Certainly not. Westwich is very dull for young people, I suspect. I did not grow up here so I can only speculate. But I do imagine I would find my own young self on the road to London eventually- be it temporary or permanent-" Leamas winked at this part, thinking he had made himself a joke. "If I were young, of course. Now I am old, Inspector, and quite satisfied in my settled state and situation."

Inspector Foxglove remained silent and thoughtful.

"Do you, Inspector, consider Westwich to be dull at your age? Of course not. You are ready, like me, to settle down and find some certitude in your daily life."

Foxglove nodded as he listened.

"You and I, you were right, we are very much the same. In outlook, in profession, in consideration of our place in life." Father Leamas said.

***

Two figures in the street; each discerning the other and otherwise occupied in thought until they come upon an intersection of their paths. Courtesy and the desire to preserve one's own dignity prevented the otherwise inevitable collision. Neither Inspector Foxglove or Penelope Pimsleur had expected to see the other in the street just that way though they both, to any passerby, were merely being polite.

"Ms Pimsleur. Pardon me- I was lost in thought and did not perceive your approach!" Foxglove said.

"Pardon me, Inspector! I was lost in thoughts of my own." Penelope said.

They regarded each other- clearly reluctant to let go of their respective trains of thought.

"Ms Pimsleur, have you only just arrived from London? I beg your pardon again. I heard you had left for London, but there was some ancillary suggestion it might have been a permanent move and not a visit?" Foxglove said.

"Only a visit, Inspector. I went to see my sister, who had taken a position there." Penelope said.

"I see. Of course. And how is Ms Hildegard?" Foxglove said.

"She is well, thank you, Inspector. She is quite well. Her situation is, though not what we dream of, certainly is stable and caring and I am very glad for her." Penelope said.

"I am glad to hear that. And how did you find London?" Foxglove said.

"My sister is almost certainly made for the big city life and all its diversions- I, for one, am glad to be home in Westwich." Penelope said.

"Did you see anyone else there, Ms Pimsleur?" Foxglove said.

This question seemed to catch Penelope off guard.

"No. No one." She considered. "Although, now you mention it." Penelope said.

"Yes?" Foxglove said.

"One of the days, my sister and I were taking a walk. We had gone further, I think, than we intended. And we found ourselves in a neighborhood she did not recognize- short as her time has been. We decided we didn't know the way and thought we had best turn exactly around and walk the opposite direction we were facing. We did so very abruptly and turned around just in time to see a man, or, only his shadow, disappear in to a little shop. It didn't seem odd that a man would go into a shop or even that a man would go into a shop, coincidentally, just as we were turning around. What was most certainly odd was that neither of us had noticed the man before- you would have to be there but the street was one where, we thought, we would have noticed someone else and certainly a man dressed as he. We walked past the shop and glanced in to see him but we saw no one." Penelope said.

"This man, was he familiar to you? Is that why you looked for him?" Foxglove said.

"No. He as entirely unfamiliar to the both of us. That was why we looked." Penelope said.

"You mean to say that you saw a man you did not recognize and felt compelled to discover him?" Foxglove said.

"Yes. Hmm, yes. I suppose that is what we did." Penelope said.

"Well, I am sorry you did not meet an old friend- I always enjoy running into old friends in the city." Foxglove said.

"Old friend, Inspector? It is funny you mention that. You know that here in Westwich, there is not a large population and the chances of having old friends in other places is extremely rare. But now that you mention it, it was strange." Penelope said.

"What was strange, Ms Pimsleur?" Foxglove said.

"What was strange- what was very strange indeed- was that as we walked home from that very shop (and we did find our way home just fine) was that we would on occasion glance behind us to see whether we might see again the man we did not know who disappeared into the shop..." Penelope said.

"And did you?" Foxglove said.

"No. Not even once, Inspector." Penelope said.

Foxglove waited for her to finish the thought until he realized she had finished the thought.

"So, you did not see the man you did not know?" Foxglove said.

"Only the one time, Inspector." She leaned in. "Don't you think that is suspicious?"

"Oh, entirely suspicious Ms Pimsleur. I am glad you had no more adventures such as that during your stay." Foxglove said.

"Adventures- no. But revelations, yes. It was a profitable visit, to say the least." Penelope said.

"That is good news, Ms Pimsleur!" Foxglove said.

"I suppose, Inspector." Penelope said.

"Well, Ms Pimsleur, you must excuse me. I have an appointment." Foxglove said.

"As do I, Inspector." Penelope said.

"Good day, Ms Pimsleur." Foxglove said.

"Good day, Inspector." Penelope said.

They each took a step in the same direction, then another. They both halted, smiling and gesturing for the other to resume. They were at an impasse.

"Ms Pimsleur, let us resolve this. I am going in the direction of the Blankenship estate. Which way are you going?" Foxglove said.

"I am also going to the Blankenship estate, Inspector." Penelope said.

"Ah! Then we are not at cross purposes! Let us each join the other and walk together to the Blankenships." Foxglove said.

"Inspector, I will not walk that distance or direction with a gentleman, but I will walk that distance and direction with an officer of the law." Penelope said. "Do we agree?"

"Well then, by all means, let us proceed." Foxglove said.

"It makes a difference, Inspector, knowing there is a capable and courageous officer watching over our town." Penelope said matter of factly.

They arrived at the Blankenships and were let in by the young maid, who was very surprised to see Penelope back again. But when they were announced, Penelope was called in first to see Mr Blankenship, as if she was expected. This surprised Foxglove, who had assumed she would be visiting with Miss Blankenship.

This left Foxglove alone in the study for some time to contemplate the case and lay it out in his mind before seeking the assistance of Mr Blankenship on a certain matter. It bothered him, and he would have willingly said so to a listening ear, to seek assistance from one such as Niles Blankenship but sometimes one had to engage a criminal mind to catch a criminal mind, he would have said. Besides, he really thought the Blankenships had the most comfortable chairs in the neighbourhood.

Foxglove reflected on the case at hand. A series of robberies necessitates his arrival and involvement in Westwich. There are no clues and no hard suspects. Everything is relatively quiet for the investigation- has the crime passed or is this the calm before the storm? Then the thundering revelation that Mr Rempart is mixed up the Devil's Elbow affair- his two companions and conspirators in that incident are dead and now the intentions of Orton Black are becoming clear.

Interview with Father Leamas

Mr Rempart would be the third and final piece of the Devil's Elbow puzzle- which is surely why he orchestrated events to make Foxglove an eyewitness to the crime. But in Orton Black's audacity on brining Foxglove in, it was also a braggadocio, believing he could pull off the crime without being caught and humiliating the law in the process. It was surely Orton Black's intention now to discover the identity of Mr Rempart, murder him as he murdered the other two, and take as much of the fortune as he could.

The question, from an investigative point of view, would be whether Black has identified Rempart, and if so, when does he intend to strike?

Inspector Foxglove was contemplating this very question of timing when he was summoned, and he rose to follow the young maid into Niles Blankenship's study. When he entered, Penelope was already gone and Blankenship sat behind his desk with a dazed look. He did not appear to notice Foxglove's arrival or announcement by the young maid. Foxglove spoke first,

"Mr Blankenship?" Foxglove said.
Niles Blankenship gave a start.

"Inspector!" He smiled broadly- the garish change from shock to glee resembled a crocodile. "Congratulate me, Inspector! Penelope Pimsleur has been fortunate enough to accept my proposal of marriage!"

In reverse of Mr Blankenship, Inspector Foxglove's smile turned to shock.

"I beg your pardon?" Foxglove said.

"It's quite true, Inspector. We are to be married at week's end." Mr Blankenship said.

"I am shocked, Mr Blankenship. I, er, congratulate you. When last we spoke, you said it would be charity to do so?" Foxglove said.

"I did, Inspector. I did indeed." Blankenship giggled. "But she has a dowry in trust which will put all that to right."

"A dowry to put it right?" Foxglove said.

"And then some, Inspector! And then some!" Blankenship said, crowing. Foxglove couldn't decide now if he was a crocodile or a rooster.

So this was what had become of the Pimsleur family- devastated and destitute. The elder daughter forced to work in London for relatives. The younger daughter, her one-time suitor now a fugitive and the cause of their troubles, forced to marry the local villain, at the cost of her future and her family's. The Pimsleurs, once a proud and generous family, now had shame to pile upon shame. It didn't seem likely they would ever lift their heads again.

They, the Pimsleurs and their troubles, were collateral damage to Orton Black's scheme. Had Black gone too far? Foxglove knew himself, from personal experience, that Black would say he hadn't yet gone far enough.

19 THE STRANGE SUMMIT

In Which, the Continued Harassments of the Vagabonds Compel Foxglove to Meet With Them and Demand an Explanation

Ms Penelope Pimsleur was to marry Mr Niles Blankenship in one week's time. There is enough to consider in that one statement for an entire chapter. But we will not take up the entire chapter with such contemplations.

First, there is a deep and abiding affection we have for Ms Penelope Pimsleur and her family. They are an upstanding and once-respected family largely responsible for the majority of the charitable notions in Westwich and its surrounding neighborhood. As such, they are an elevated family and Penelope herself was long considered the jewel of the family. Hildegard, of course, was not considered a mean second place, she had virtues all her own but if we are being fair and honest and keeping it between ourselves, Penelope was still the favorite.

Secondly, the tragedy of the Pimsleur family, so unexpected and devastating, set the town on end, so to speak, about fairness and righteousness and had them all wondering if there mightn't be some secret sin the Pimsleur family was hiding to be in such a state?

Thirdly, we must consider the villainous nature of the Blankenship siblings. We cannot consider one sibling without the other. Taken in comparison with the Pimsleur siblings, despite the significant age difference, they would not be considered on the same plane in worth or moral character. Even the recent decline of the Pimsleurs could hardly offset the differences- unless there really were a secret sin the Pimsleurs were hiding.

Fourthly, there was most certainly no secret sin being hidden by the Pimsleurs.

***

On the Monday before the wedding, news came to Foxglove that Caleb Cheswick had left London and disappeared completely. Nothing had been seen or heard from him after a careful combing of all the hovels and holes which Foxglove's contacts could think of or imagine.

"Surely he heard about Penelope and Niles-" Foxglove thought. "And since he is innocent he has abandoned our plan? He means to ruin the wedding, at least."

A telegram arrived for Foxglove, from Cheswick, confirming this very thing;

"Leaving London today. Stop. Must prevent wedding. Stop."

With this news then, Foxglove began deputizing people in Westwich to actively watch the roads into Westwich and the surrounding neighborhood. He didn't need or want a proper roadblock, but it certainly was to his advantage to know when and where Cheswick would show up.

The Vagabond question, too, had been growing in his mind like a rain cloud- it had now become dark and ominous and he would have to address it. He didn't think they would shelter Cheswick exactly, but they may aid him in some way. They were certainly the unknown quantity in the neighbourhood, as far as his professional understanding went.

The main difficulty was the public opinion- that is, that Cheswick was a criminal and his appearance would likely lead to violence by the public. Also, he needed Cheswick to be gone in order to strike the real target of Orton Black.

He decided his hand had been forced. He had begun recruiting strong and sturdy men from the town and deputising them. He further deputised Mr Niles Blankenship to lead them as a sort of patrol unit for the surrounding neighborhood. The more eyes the better, he recruited young men with sharp eyes and nothing better to do to keep watch from strategic places in the town, at the various crossroads, and most certainly on the road from Brakton, where the train stopped.

Mr Blankenship, thrilled with the idea of ordering men around, jumped at the chance to be in charge. At his sister's suggestion, he began referring to the men as Foxglove's Brigade and at Foxglove's suggestion trimmed it to, simply, the Brigade. The headquarters for the Brigade was established at the Blankenship home, complete with a guard at the front gate.

***

On Tuesday, Arthur Denton, he of the newly formed Brigade, pulled a drag from his fourteenth cigarette of the morning and watched the smoke roll out from his nose as he exhaled in staccato bursts. The combinations and permutations of amusement available to a chain smoker are legion and young Arthur was a master of his craft, having been smoking nearly non-stop since he was twelve. Standing around- as he had been now for several hours- had never been a problem for him, so long as his parents weren't around to tell him to take that wretched thing out of your mouth.

None of which is to say he wasn't paying attention to the landscape under his watch as a member of the newly formed and deputised Foxglove

Brigade (as they had begun calling themselves). He had been assigned the crossroad of the South Road and Ancillary, off of the southeast corner of the moor. It was the furthest post the Brigade had established under Foxglove's orders and Arthur Denton, all of fifteen years old, was considered the spry one and thus best equipped to make the trip out to this far end of the surrounding neighbourhood, his storm cloud black lungs notwithstanding.

The storm clouds intermittently burst now and again as he stood watch and a devilish hacking and coughing would ensue, interrupting whatever he was presently engaged in for measures of time and inconvenient sequels which would have been enough to put Mr Rampert's patience to the test. Arthur's eyes watered with the effort and he expectorated extensively. He cursed the damp weather for his cough and promised himself someday he would move to the Indias where it was always dry and sunny and smoke to his heart's uninterrupted content.

Had he realised how long the shadowed figure had been standing in plain sight, he might have also had the wherewithal to reconsider a number of various aspects of his life. As it was, it took him by surprise (as would a great many more predictable things in the course of his life; happily, none of which concerns our story even remotely). Across the road from his post, just at the edge of the wood, a Vagabond clearly stood. The shadowy figure appeared to be regarding him with feigned indifference, since the moment they made eye-contact, the figure squinted at him, then melted into the wood across the road.

It had not been an illusion- the type of thing the trees and shadows can sometimes create. It had not been a figment of his imagination- the type of thing he was generally unacquainted with. It had been a real, living, breathing Vagabond- the type of thing he had seen perhaps once or twice in his short life. "See and Scoot" were his orders. He had Seen. Now it was time to Scoot. He took off running toward the crossroad and made the tight turn to head north on the Ancillary toward the Blankenship Estate, where the Foxglove Brigade was headquartered.

***

With the Foxglove Brigade (as they were now calling themselves) strategically in place, all there was to do was wait. They didn't have to wait long. Niles Blankenship was seated in his study- the temporary headquarters of the Brigade- when in burst young Arthur Denton, shouting and coughing. Niles Blankenship, who imagined this was how the military actually did things and thus not concerned he hadn't been announced, leapt to his feet.

"At attention, Brigadesman!" Blankenship shouted.

Young Arthur saluted with the wrong hand. Niles returned it.

"Mr Blankenship! I have a sighting to report!" Arthur was still shouting.

Mr Blankenship, who imagined this was how the military actually did things, shouted, "Report, Denton!"

"I saw a Vagabond, Mr Blankenship!"

"What! Where?!" Mr Blankenship said.

"At my post- across the road in the wood!" young Arthur said.

Mr Blankenship, who somehow imagined this was how the military actually did things, stood stock still, absorbing the news. "This is serious." he declared. He had a realisation just beginning to bud in his intellect when in burst another Brigadesman.

"Mr Blankenship! I've seen a Vagabond, with my own eyes!" the young man shouted, unwittingly competing with Arthur in volume.

"At your post, Selfridge?" Blankenship demanded.

"Yes, Mr Blankenship. I was at my post and saw a Vagabond." the young man named Selfridge said.

"What happened?" said Blankenship, who imagined this was how the military actually did things. Neither he nor Selfridge had saluted.

"I was standing at my post, just like I was told, and I saw a Vagabond." Selfridge said.

Mr Blankenship pounded the desk. "That's good enough for me!" He said, imagining this was how the military actually did things. He called a third Brigadesman in; a secretary in charge of secretarial things, but primarily someone to whom Blankenship could announce his plans and actions to.

""I am going to Foxglove to report this." he said. He turned back to Denton and Selfridge. "Back to your posts, men."

Denton and Selfridge, grateful to finally be acknowledged as men by a man, crowded each other out the door. Niles Blankenship was only a step behind them, eager to make his first report to Inspector Foxglove and impress him with his ability to put a reconnaissance together and organise it to such a quick result. His sister stopped him.

"Niles, where are you going? Will you be back for tea?" she said.

"The Empire, Prunaprismia! The Empire!" Niles Blankenship said.

***

Inspector Foxglove was having a quiet morning. He had commissioned Blankenship knowing there was no one in town so eager for authority, however false, and in the meantime worried about Cheswick- in an unknown location and apparently not eager for authority. It was easier to handle men who clearly wanted something. Niles Blankenship was as predictable as a worker ant but Caleb Cheswick, he was a different. With those thoughts in mind, Foxglove heard Blankenship arrive.

"Inspector," Niles Blankenship said. He sort-of saluted. The man he addressed, sitting at the desk, who really had been in the military once, didn't care. "I have two confirmed reports of sightings. One to the southeast and one to the north-northwest."

He had Foxglove's attention and was very pleased with the attentiveness.

"Two sightings? Are we following him?" Inspector Foxglove said.

"Following him?" Blankenship was taken aback. "No, we're not following anyone. We were told to report."

"Well, yes. When was he spotted? Just now?" Foxglove said.

"Yes- approximately, anyway. They were spotted and the spotters- the brigadesmen- reported back immediately." Blankenship said.

"They? You said 'they' were spotted. Who's they?" Foxglove said.

"They? The Vagabonds. Two of them. We spotted them and they were reported to me. I came here right away to let you know." Blankenship said.

Silence.

"Mr Blankenship. Your men are on the lookout for one Caleb Cheswick. Not the Vagabonds. Has there been any sighting of Caleb Cheswick?" Foxglove said.

Blankenship vaguely sensed something was wrong.

"No. There has been no sighting of Mr Cheswick." he looked hopefully at Foxglove. "But we will be on the lookout for him!" Blankenship said.

"Yes, Mr Blankenship. Please do." Foxglove said.

***

Young Arthur Denton had been back at his post most of the day when he made his second sighting of the day. A Vagabond, much like before, had suddenly appeared in the shadows across the road from his post. The Vagabond eyed him and he eyed the Vagabond. Arthur put down his burning desire to run and report to Brigade HQ that he had spotted another Vagabond but he remembered in time his instructions from Mr Blankenship himself, that is, "We are not interested in Vagabonds. We are interested in Caleb Cheswick." So Arthur remained alert and, at least outwardly, composed. And ignored the Vagabond in the lengthening shadows- it was late afternoon by now.

But the Vagabond did not melt into the shadows. The Vagabond just stood there, watching Arthur. Arthur averted his eyes and studiously looked at anything but the Vagabond. Each tree along the road to the right of the Vagabond eyeing him; one, two, three, four, five... he glanced back at the Vagabond inadvertently. No change there. Back to the trees. Onetwothreefourfive, six, seven, eight...

Arthur Denton couldn't take it anymore.

"We are not interested in you!" he said. The shout was clearly loud enough to be heard across the road- no more than twenty meters away.

The Vagabond regarded him silently, then made a motion with its hand.

"Can't be distracted! I'm on post!" Young Arthur said. He was perilously curious to talk to the Vagabond, since he had never seen one this close before. He was both terrified and nearly drawn across the road by an inner Arthur who really wanted to live in the woods off of magic and his wits alone like the Vagabonds.

Arthur's resolve to stay on post was nearly defeated by the complacent Vagabond, when suddenly his fear rose up as the Vagabond stepped out of the shadows and approached him directly, walking on bare feet.

The Vagabond- the boy, as Arthur could now plainly see- was perhaps nine or ten years old and dressed in the colours of the wood, or moor, where he lived. A rough belt at his waist held a longknife. Sandy hair stuck out at strange places from under the wide brim of his hat which was further adorned with a long pheasant feather.

Arthur Denton had no weapon and no feather in his cap and was clearly overmatched by this sprite from the deep wood. Then an inspiration came to him. Probably the instinct to avoid death but it felt like inspiration. Arthur had nearly swallowed his cigarette when the Vagabond boy approached him and suddenly it struck him to him to offer the stranger a smoke. How bizarre it was, Arthur realised. He might well die by the longknife and be dragged off and buried in the woods and his clothes sold off for liquor (these were the usual Vagabond stories) but all he could think of was to share a smoke with the boy.

His hand shook as much as his smile as he held out the cigarette to the Vagabond boy, who regarded it much as he had regarded Arthur himself. He was close enough now to reach out a hand to accept the offered gift. Taking the cigarette from Arthur, the boy looked it over in close examination, up and down, then crushed it with his little hand. At the same instant, and seemingly to Arthur from nowhere, he whisked out a long pipe and stuffed the crushed cigarette into the bowl of the pipe. The Vagabond boy stood silently eyeing Arthur.

Arthur stared at the boy and wondered where the pipe had come from.

The boy looked harder at Arthur.

Arthur didn't feel threatened. The boy was looking fiercely at him now- but it wasn't threatening, it was...

"A light?" the Vagabond boy said.

"Crickets!" Arthur said. He fumbled for his matches and wasted three before he could compose himself enough to hand a lit match to the other, who quickly lit his pipe and stuffed the burnt end of the match into the bowl as well.

They smoked together for a minute.

Then two.

No one spoke.

Arthur felt he was partaking in an ancient ritual. The brotherhood of knights-errant meeting by chance on the highway, or a friendly peasant and one of Robin's Merry Men well met at the sign of the Blue Boar and sharing a secret from the sheriff. The first meeting of two civilisations in the early world of tribes and painted warriors and the desperate competition of foraging and hunting. Arthur felt he might have helped avoid those ugly wars, a brave arbitrator conducting peace pipe ceremonies and reasoning with the chieftains, showing them the backwardness of their ways. He would show them how to live peacefully, harmoniously, together making a new and mighty civilisation of progress. He would teach them fire. They would have to reward him with gold and jewels and a hut of his own and the two once-warring tribes would fight over whose princess he would marry and he would have to make the difficult choice of which royal heart to break. There would be much girlish weeping. Perhaps the ancient world allowed more than one wife for the very powerful- he would tolerate their backwardness with a kindly gaze and rule them with an iron fist.

"Now we speak." the Vagabond boy said.

"Right." Arthur said.

"Your people are looking for Caleb Cheswick." the Vagabond said. It really wasn't even a question.

"Yes, that's right." Arthur said.

"We have seen him upon the moor. He has trespassed upon our age-old land and I come to warn you." the Vagabond boy said.

"Warn us of what?" Arthur said.

"We will kill him if he strays into our land. He belongs to you and he is your responsibility. Take care of him. Protect him from us. That is our warning." the Vagabond boy said.

Arthur Denton was now too stimulated with thoughts and experiences to stand still. He once again took off running up the road, toward the crossroad and then making a quick turn north up the Ancillary to the Brigade headquarters where Niles Blankenship would be pleased to receive news about the sighting of Caleb Cheswick.

The Vagabond boy smiled and just like that the road was empty again.

***

Torches were lit in a circle on the edge of the open moor and the forest. Foxglove had come and stood at the ancient boundary and waited until a Vagabond delegation had approached him. He quickly explained his need to speak to their chief and would be pleased to wait there as long as necessary for him. So he had waited for an hour or so, Niles Blankenship with him and an assortment of the Brigadesmen (including Arthur Denton) which Blankenship had insisted on for protection.

The Strange Summit

They had waited until after dark and then, as if by magic, torchlight had appeared on the edge of the wood. Torches, perhaps two dozen, lit simultaneously from periphery to periphery. They converged on Foxglove and the others and surrounded them. There they stood in the center of the ring of fire and out of the darkness beyond the torches a single figure advanced to stand with them.

It was a boy. Maybe twelve years of age. He sounded older. More authoritative than most whom Foxglove had dealt with in the Westwich neighbourhood.

"You wished to speak with the Chief of the Vagabonds." the boy said. It wasn't really a question. Clearly, he was the chief and leader of them all. *You are speaking to him* would have been unnecessary.

"Chief, my name is Foxglove." Foxglove said. This is not how Arthur would have brought peace, Arthur thought.

"A curious name, Inspector." the Chief said.

"You're right, I am Inspector Foxglove. You have told us that you have seen Caleb Cheswick upon your moor. He is a fugitive of justice." Foxglove said.

"We have seen him. But he is not with us. We warned you we would kill him if we saw him." the Chief said.

"I must ask for your assistance in apprehending him." Foxglove said.

A diminutive boy now stepped into the ring. "You wished to speak to the Chief. Then you must speak to me." the little boy said. The older, much bigger boy, retreated into the shadows.

The Brigadesmen gasped.

Foxglove fixed his gaze down on the real Chief.

"Chief. I must ask for your assistance in apprehending this Caleb Cheswick." Foxglove said.

"Then you must make an agreement with us!" the Chief said.

"I understand. What are the terms?" Foxglove said. Arthur thought he was doing better now.

"You must swear fealty to our tribe, and pay a tribute." the Chief said.

"I am not authorised to hold such negotiations. I am a visiting officer of the law- I am not asking on behalf of this town. I am asking on behalf of the goodness of all people." Foxglove said.

Instantly, the little boy disappeared and another boy took his place.

"You wished to speak with the Chief of the Vagabonds. You must speak with me, then." he said, more convincingly than either of the other two boys.

The Brigadesmen had never imagined such a dramatic turn of events.

"I need your help in apprehending Caleb Cheswick." Foxglove said.

"Then you must speak with me!" said one of the torch-bearers, and handed his torch to the third boy- now clearly not the Chief after all. "Bring it out!"

This last line was directed to the shadows and from out of there, came a Vagabond carrying two steaming drinking mugs.

"We will drink together our future capture of Caleb Cheswick- the fugitive and vigilante!" the true Chief said.

"HEAR, HEAR!" all the Vagabonds said, raising their torches.

One of the mugs was handed to Foxglove, the other to the Chief. The stood facing one another and put the mugs to their lips. Both tilted the mugs back until the liquid spilled over the edges. Foxglove spluttered as he tasted the concoction- too late to realise the Chief had been aping and pouring his mug out on the ground as Foxglove realised he was drinking hot mud. With that, the torches went out all at once and the men were left alone in the sudden darkness. All they heard was the hooting and laughing of the swiftly retreating Vagabonds.

20 THE WEATHER CHANGES

The previous night, Tuesday, in the immediate aftermath of the single most embarrassing professional experience of his life, Inspector Foxglove suggested someone who "knows the area" lead the way back to the road nearest the place in the moor where they were. There were more than a couple men who fit this description and they were all soon headed in the right direction, guided by the disembodied voices of their companions under a dark and moonless night sky.

It was in everyone's best interest that evening they could not see each other stumbling over every rock, root and tuft of grass their feet could find- although, of course, had they been able to see, that would also have been to everyone's advantage. Either way, as Arthur Denton considered it, one had to admit a certain level of convenience. He did not share this insight with anyone and the curses emanating out of the darkness on either hand were a steady reminder not to.

Niles Blankenship, for his part, was still in deep thought regarding the seemingly endless hierarchy of the Vagabond culture and wondered at their sophistication. He himself was now a brigade leader and the accompanying perspective opened his eyes mightily to the events of the evening. He envied the Vagabonds their coordination at the fire ring. It had seemed to him to be both entirely spontaneous and manifestly orchestrated all at the same time. It was baffling, infuriating and entirely beautiful to see in action. He uttered a few words in reflection to which those nearby in the dark asked if he was alright, thinking he had gotten into a particularly nasty thorn bush, judging solely by his choice of verbiage.

It did not enter the mind of a single man among them to actually speak to Foxglove about the summit with the Vagabonds or the way in which it had ended. It was wholly to their credit. At last the group came to the road and they turned all as one man toward town. On they went, some leaving here or there along the road as they came to their own homes, until it was only Foxglove. He stood before the door of the Bull & Bear, in a rare moment of uncertainty. He was drawn by the idea of washing out the taste in his mouth but repulsed by the notion of having to explain anything. In that moment, in the aftermath of such an episode, the very strangest thought entered his mind:

I wonder if Orton Black would go in and have a drink, or would he only walk on?

Foxglove shook his head and abandoned the question before a perfunctory answer could manifest. There was real work to be done, beginning tomorrow morning.

***

Thus, Wednesday morning came and the work which Foxglove did not want to do at all had become entirely necessary. It was time to organize the Brigade into an actual manhunt. The difficulty of this development was multifaceted.

One. He knew Caleb Cheswick to be perfectly innocent and actually, quite hapless.

Two. He knew the town believed Caleb Cheswick to be a fugitive and a scoundrel. If anyone saw him, it would be the end.

Three. The manhunt had to be organised in such a way as to satisfy the town he really was trying to apprehend Cheswick.

Four. The manhunt had to be organised in such a way as to not actually apprehend Cheswick too soon.

Five. The manhunt had to be organised in such a way as to facilitate the real purpose of his being in Westwich in the first place, that is, the target of Orton Black.

These facts required responses.

To the first, Caleb Cheswick might be perfectly innocent (he really was an innocent, wasn't he?) but his ignorant attempt to intervene in the marriage between Penelope and Niles was threatening the ultimate goal of Orton Black.

To the second, the Brigade would be his buffer against the town- if they could catch Cheswick first, then he need not fear the whole town and hopefully the Brigade would follow orders when the time came.

To the third, he decided this would be easy enough with regular reporting.

To the fourth, this could merely be a matter of timing. Once Orton Black was discovered, Cheswick's innocence would be evident.

To the fifth... well, that was the trick, wasn't it? This manhunt wasn't very likely to capture Orton Black.

***

Providing an unexpected backdrop to the planning of Foxglove, was the rapid deterioration of the weather situation. They had had rain and a few storms already that year but this was quickly shaping up to be a long, wet, windy week, to say the least. The feel on the stiffening air was one of impending doom, as if a real storm was headed their way. And in fact, it was.

It would be years before meteorologically inclined historians put all the pieces together, but a rough summation for our purposes was this; an enormous weather system was coming northwest off of the continent, and mating with a relatively lesser, but far more temperamental system, which had been knocking about over the North Sea (already famous for its disregard for the personal safety of sailors or the monetary values of their cargo).

These two systems did not immediately cojoin. No. They first stirred up a maelstrom out over the open North Sea and then, like two drunken sailors in a wharfman's bar, they decided in an instant they were best of friends and went in search of a third party to take their newfound friendship out on. They- now one single storm system- saw the defunct little harbor town of Wasteon and went at it full bore.

A really strong and determined North Sea storm could raise the coastal water levels and overwhelm local preventative measures, then ride that flooded wave deep inland. These were the kinds of storms for which the elaborate dike systems of the Netherlands, Germany and Denmark were built, to prevent the devastating floods just such a storm could bring. It seemed this storm had done its research- it headed instead directly for English shores, where such systems were not in place.

Beyond that and inland, Westwich was still protected by twelve miles of countryside- but it was largely open and low lying land. Marshes, moors and fields with only occasional (and very small) bits of forest. It was just the sort of country a really vicious water-borne storm dreams about and this open country led straight to Westwich. It was Wednesday and the first clouds were darkening the sky. By Thursday night, or Friday morning, it would be on Westwich in full force. For now, it was only a slight increase in the winds from the sea, and the cloud cover.

***

Foxglove had been privy to the mechanics of many a manhunt in his career and in this case, the object of the hunt was much less experienced and wily than the previous. Though it was impossible to cover the entire neighbourhood of Westiwch at once, a systematic approach combined with proper safeguards would allow Foxglove and the Brigade to sweep the area with something like efficiency. Foxglove would divide the map into zones and then zone by zone they could eliminate the hiding places available to Caleb Cheswick.

This was quite ludicrous to Foxglove, this effort being made toward Cheswick, but now it was necessary. The young man, not knowing any better and thinking quite selfishly, had thrown a considerable difficulty into the larger operation.

Foxglove laid out the map of the neighborhood on his desk and began cordoning it off in the simplest manner with a ruler and pen- a grid with alpha-numeric coordinates which, when he was finished with it, gave him a series of boxes all with labels such A-3 and F-2 and so on. He called Blankenship in and showed him the map, instructing him on how to divide the Brigade into the right number of men to check each box, and then leave enough pairs of eyes to be sure Cheswick didn't merely slip around them into a box already 'cleared'.

This was not especially complicated and or even difficult but Foxglove had his reservations about the capabilities of the men Blankenship had recruited to his Brigade. These reservations, however, worked in his favor since the manhunt couldn't be too effective or it might actually work and then he would have to deal with arresting Cheswick and all the general headache associated with arresting an innocent man. This shadow play was getting nearly out of hand, he thought.

Blankenship, with his new orders, now gathered his men and by noon, they were making their way to their assigned cordons, or, boxes, according to the map. Today, they would only be making a general and cursory sweep of the entire map, making note of any hiding places along the way, so that the next day they might target more specifically.

The manhunt, for all intents and purposes, was begun.

21 THE APOCAPLYPSE OF CALEB CHESWICK

Thursday morning came with a dim sunrise and rain and the rain continued all day.

The Brigade had been forming up all morning to do their proper sweep for the day- the last of them had marched out hours earlier when Foxglove had a wholly unexpected visitor. A woman, a housemaid it was evident, arrived in her raincoat with her bonnet hardly tied and her boots covered in mud. It hadn't rained enough for all that mud, Foxglove observed, unless she had walked a fair distance to accumulate it all- he was exactly right.

The poor housemaid, whose expression was one of certain anxiety, was asking for the Inspector- clearly not remembering his face in her distress.

"It is I, ma'am. I am Inspector Foxglove." Foxglove said.

"Oh Inspector! It's awful!" she said. "You must help!"

"Dear woman, what is it? Foxglove said.

"It's Mr Rampert, Inspector! You must come!" the housemaid said.

"What has happened, ma'am. Tell me at once!" Foxglove said.

"He's gone, Inspector! He's gone!" she said.

Foxglove read the distress in her eyes and decided he needn't trouble her with questions like "are you sure?" or "have you looked in the dining room" or other such nonsense. He saw at once something really was amiss. He plucked his hat up and flung on his long macintosh.

"We will go in my phaeton, ma'am! Come with me at once!" he commanded and off they went the moment the buggy was brought around.

They arrived minutes later at the the Huffington Estate. Foxglove pulled the phaeton nearly right to the front door and a steward stumbled out to take the horse's head while Foxglove helped the housemaid down onto the steps of the house. Once inside, he deposited his wet outerwear into the waiting arms of another servant. He turned to the housemaid again,

"Please assemble everyone in the kitchen at once. I must question them quickly." Foxglove said.

The housemaid, nodded to the others standing about and off they fanned (awfully efficiently, Foxglove saw) to the outbuildings while she herself went to the kitchen and began ringing the housebells for assembly.

Soon, Foxglove was surrounded by the staff servants of the Huffington-In-Box estate.

"Good morning, I am here to begin an investigation to find Mr Rempart. If any one of you has something important to disclose, please speak up. Otherwise, I will question you all in turn and discover for myself all I need." Foxglove said.

"Mr Fox-, er, Inspector Foxglove?" one man said.

"Yes, sir?" Foxglove said.

"Would you like to see the scene of the crime?" the man said.

"Crime? There is no crime to discover that we know of. A man is missing- that is enough. What scene?" Foxglove said, trying to control the situation but then realising the man might be onto something. It was not necessarily a crime- but it was certainly no coincidence, either.

"His bedroom, sir. He was last seen in his bedroom." the man said.

"Ah, last night I take it, as he went to bed?" Foxglove said.

The man was astounded. "Yes sir, that is exactly it."

"Does Mr Rempart often go to bed at night- and disappear into his bedroom? In other words, did anything different at all happen last night?" Foxglove said.

"No sir- it's just as you said. The same every night." the man said. Several others nodded.

"Well, then. I'll just start questioning you all individually. Please form a line to the study and I'll interview each of you in turn. Thank you." Foxglove said.

With the interviews done quickly and efficiently, Foxglove began his inspection of Mr Rampert's bedroom. He started high and worked all the way down to the floor covering. No article, appliance or furnishment unexamined. Then, when there was nothing left to see- he had found nothing; Foxglove lifted the pillow off the bed and there, under the pillow, was a note.

My Dear Inspector Foxglove,
    How coincidental we should meet here in Westwich! I have kidnapped Mr Rempart, whom we both know to be more than he lets on. And you will find me, as always, unfindable!
-Orton Black

Foxglove dropped the note from his now-shaking hand

This was more than a kidnapping. This was a thunderclap over Foxglove's head. This was a game beyond what he had imagined. The note was signed Orton Black, but Foxglove knew the truth. It hit him like an unexpected blow. Up until this moment,

Foxglove believed Caleb Cheswick was exactly as he appeared and proclaimed- a university student, thrust into a role as constable, an innocent. A young man in the wrong place at the wrong time. But now he saw the truth of the matter as plain as the note. This was a revelation of the highest order. His mind was spinning, working, pushing through the fog, searching the darkest places of his mind for an answer and from that dark place came the face of Caleb Cheswick.

Resolve came to him. His fists formed, rock hard and determined. Now he knew who he was dealing with. He paused, and looked down at the note again, and the revelation of Caleb Cheswick swept over him. *Orton Black will not win this contest*, he thought grimly, *Justice, that fearsome entity, will win the day.*

22 ORTON BLACK AT LAST!

In the night, the storm from the coast had met Westwich head-on and poured its fury out in torrential rain, house-shaking thunder and lightning strikes had started at least one fire in the neighbourhood, though the rain conveniently kept it contained, smoldering, then put it out completely. Wind, persistently strong and gusting enough to take down limbs and uproot trees in low-lying areas where the soil around the roots was saturated and unable to withstand the onslaught.

The manhunt had been unsuccessful thus far but that was no surprise to Foxglove, now he knew Caleb Cheswick's real identity. The people of Westwich would never catch him unless he wanted to be caught. Foxglove realized he would have to track down Cheswick himself.

Foxglove looked over the map. He still had lookouts in key positions which would limit Cheswick a little. The storm, however, had reduced the ranks of willing participants of the Brigade. His lookouts could not be fully trusted. The headquarters having been transferred to the priory, Miss Blankenship having tired of cleaning up after the muddy boots of the Brigadesmen going to and coming fro.

More people began filling the priory from the town. Not only Brigadesmen but now ordinary townsfolk, seeking shelter from the storm and, perhaps, to pray. It became necessary to herd these visitors toward the front of the priory, where they sat in the pews or on the power steps of the small platform. Pews were reserved toward the back for the Brigadesmen to rest, hanging their wet things on the pegs at the very back of the room to dry out while making a puddle on the floor below- this was swept out the door at intervals by a woman with a broom who had started the day sitting in the pew but who had become less comfortable sitting as the day progressed.

Most any one of those locals from Westwich, those who had grown up in the area, would have been surprised to learn just how well Foxglove knew the Westich and neighbouring areas for himself. He seemed to have, in his short time there, picked up almost preternaturally the lay of the land. He would, if asked, attribute it to long years of experience and hard work. The criminal, he would say, has weeks or months to scout a location for a crime and learn its strengths, weaknesses, vulnerabilities and attitudes. It was the job of the inspector, then, to arrive and get up to speed- no, to get out ahead of the criminal in just a few days or even hours. The advantage of familiarity with a place must be taken back from the criminal in short order. But here in Westwich, Foxglove had been on the ground for several weeks now. Plenty of time, he thought to himself, to know where everything was. He really was a remarkable man.

"Mr Blankenship." Foxglove addressed the Brigade leader. "I am going out. Retain any relevant reports here- I will check in later."

"Of course, sir. But where are you going?" Blankenship said, but Foxglove had already left the room.

His first point was to head toward town- a mile or less- and see what there might be to discover at Cheswick's own lodgings. If Cheswick really was who Foxglove thought he was, there might be something in his rooms to help in either identifying him, or tracking him down, or both. The rain prevented him from seeing far, obscuring everything. He kept his head down, the brim of his hat running like a waterfall onto his boots, slogging through the mud of the road. He moved to the edge of the road, preferring the wet grass to the slow pace required on the road. He kept his hands deep in his long macintosh and wished he could smoke but he knew he would never keep it lit.

Foxglove expertly let himself into Cheswick's rooms and thoroughly ransacked it. By lunchtime, he had found nothing of note. Not a slip of paper, not whiff of a clue to reveal Cheswick's true intentions.

Just like Orton Black. Foxglove thought. It was obvious, as plain as the nose on his face, but not a single piece of hard evidence to connect them. *Genius is found in the strangest places.*

He normally would have gone to the pub for a meal now- but he had no appetite now. Cheswick was here, he had Mr Rampert hidden somewhere and he had to be found. Cheswick had grown up here and would know where to hide. Foxglove, still standing in the midst of Cheswick's rooms, crossed his arms and furrowed his brow in thought. He was reviewing every conversation, every word, he had shared with Cheswick. His observations on the moor and the Vagabonds. His comments on those who lived in town versus those who lived 'on the moor'. His observations on flora- which seemed genuine enough, but then, he had lived there his whole life.

Cheswick never talked about anyone, in specific, except the Pimsleurs. Or rather, Penelope Pimsleur. They had known each other as children, played together. What was it Cheswick had said about Miss Penelope? She had some wild and fanciful tale about the cottage on the Huffington Estate, across the road from the main residence and deep in the wood there. She said it had been haunted... that was it! Cheswick was keeping Rampert at the Huffington cottage.

He didn't know how he knew exactly, but it all came together perfectly. What did Orton Black really want? The third portion of the Devil's Elbow treasure. Who had it? Mr Rampert, the man who owned the Huffington Estate. And where else to hide an elaborate treasure than in a hidden place? It all made sense. All of it. From his arrival in Westwich to this very moment. Now Foxglove saw Cheswick plainly- and he despised what he saw.

He left the rooms and stepped once again into the rain, long strides taking him down the road- the road which would lead him to the cottage at Huffington.

Mentally pursuing the betrayal of Cheswick, he tried to determine where and when he should have realised it. He should have seen it coming, after all, he was no stranger to such subterfuge. A dozen other cities in his career had experienced just such a situation. It was nothing new. Pretend to be someone else. It was a game children played from the earliest ages. Men and women played it to win the affection of each other. Politicians played it to have their way in Parliament. Tavern owners and traders in London played it to keep business going.

But since when did botanists play at such games? He wondered.

And just like that, he knew.

There had been that one early suspicion, natural to anyone in the business of criminals and crime-stopping, that Cheswick might not be who he appeared to be. He had even asked Blankenship about Cheswick as a botanist- and Blankenship had no answer. Not that he expected him to have an answer, but now Foxglove recognised his own question for what it was; it pointed to Foxglove's suspicion, and one he should have followed up on, he now saw. The price to be paid for that oversight, so small at the time, now writ large over the entire neighbourhood of Westwich, hanging like his own doom.

Cheswick had claimed to be a botanist, studying in London. A very convenient ploy to mislead anyone in Westwich. There was really no accounting for where he had been the past several years. He might easily have been in Germany or Spain when those crimes connected to the Devil's Elbow were committed. Now Foxglove saw how he had been set up, and lured to Westwich.

It took longer than it should have, but he couldn't have risked a horse in this

horrible weather. The walk here should have worn him out, but his sense were keyed and his excitement and anticipation of the confrontation before him invigorated him. At last, Foxglove spotted the cottage. Here was the last hiding place of Caleb Cheswick. It was dark under the dense cloud cover and raining hard as ever and Foxglove, shielding his eyes from it, surveyed the area for hiding places and traps with squinted eyes. If Cheswick had Mr Rampert in that cottage, he would have to very careful how he approached. Then, in the artificial dusk of the storm, he saw a single lamp burning in the window of the cottage. He crouched in the underbrush and waited for the opportune moment.

***

Inside, Mr Rampert sat tied to the chair. The cottage was otherwise empty, except a simple bed and a small desk.

Then in walked Orton Black.

"So, Mr Rampert. Shall we begin?" Orton Black said.

Outside, the rain had slowed to a drizzle and a breeze had replaced the strong gales. The clouds had relented and allowed some of the setting sun to filter through. No one in Westwich knew, this was only the eye of the storm; the calm; and the worst was yet to come.

"It was you!" Mr Rampert said. "You killed them! You killed Francis Bixby and Peter Gallant! You murdered them and stole all they had!"

"Yes, that was me. And now I will kill you. I'll take what's left of your fortune and the name Orton Black will become a legend even as I disappear from the face of the earth!" the Master Criminal said.

"The Pimsleurs! You destroyed them too, you monster. We all trusted you!" Mr Rampert screamed.

"Well, that is how

At that very moment, the Detective burst into the room.

"Black! You are under arrest!" he said.

Orton Black spun around in surprise and sneered when he saw the Detective.

"Not likely!" he said. And he charged full bore at him.

They crashed like bulls. The Criminal and the Detective. Mr Rampert nearly feared for his life as the two struggled around the room, raining blows hard upon each other. Knocking, falling, it was all a blur to the old man, helpless as he was, and tied to the chair. The criminal had the upper hand, then the detective had it, and then Rampert wasn't certain who was winning. It seemed to go on forever. Neither man would give quarter. Neither man held back now the game was over- no more cat and mouse, no more hide and seek, no more pursuit and evade- they were locked in full mortal combat.

The brutal fight went on. The Criminal mercilessly pummelled the other with body blows, left and right, while the Detective used his length to penetrate the other's defenses. Each man wearing the blood of the other on his fists. They staggered now and again. Desperation began to set in. Each man had put on display his full arsenal, each fighter had anticipated and deflected the other's every intent, and each man had used all his tricks until only one of them had just one trick left. It was only a look- a feint- but it was all it took. Then quite suddenly the fight, so long and now so tiring, was over.

***

Back at the rectory, now temporary Brigade headquarters, the eye of the storm had long passed, and with it the calm; the storm seemed to have found a new rage. The rain slammed against the walls of the priory. The thunder was relentless. The lightning brought false daylight more often than not and the wind assailed one side, then the other, in quick and decisive turns.

At the back of the room, the door from the exterior was flung open and a figure familiar to everyone who had assembled there appeared. It was Inspector Foxglove- but something was very, very wrong. He was forcibly shoved from behind and stumbled into the room and all eyes were on him. He was wet, disheveled and his hands, clearly, were bound behind his back. He fell to his knees and in his face they read despair. The mighty champion of the law was defeated!

The next moment frightened them all the more- a bonecrack of thunder rumbled through every heart and a flash of lightning illuminated the tall man in the doorway. There stood Caleb Cheswick! He looked as worn, as wet and as haggard as Foxglove, but he wore a triumphant smile. He spread his arms wide and shouted loud enough for all of them to hear.

"So, you wanted Orton Black! Well, here he is!"

23 THE WEDDING DAY

Nobody moved or spoke a word.

They were too stunned by the sight of Inspector Foxglove in chains, too dismayed by the sight of Caleb Cheswick standing over him in triumph. But what happened next set them all talking again.

Caleb Cheswick pointed directly at Foxglove, kneeling on the floor before him and said, "This man is not Inspector Foxglove! This man is the notorious Orton Black! He has been lying to you all along! He is responsible for all the crime, all the trouble, all the mischief! He is the thief who terrorized our homes and he is the arsonist who burnt the Pimsleur estate to the ground! He meant to murder Mr Rampert but we stopped him in time!"

"Wait a moment!" someone shouted "He said YOU were Orton Black!"

Cheswick nodded in understanding.

The Wedding Day

"This is difficult to believe, I know, but let me ask you this: this man claims to be from Scotland Yard. Did he ever show you a badge?"

It was such a simple question, and regarding such a simple truth, it took them all by surprise. They blinked as one, seemingly. But when they looked at Foxglove now, they realised the truth as plainly as they saw him.

"No. We never saw any badge. No identification. No papers. Nothing to prove he was who he said he was."

"You're safe from him, now. He cannot do any more harm." Caleb Cheswick said.

Behind Cheswick, through the open door, came two more men. They were just as soaked as Cheswick. One was a small man, the other not much taller but much wider and had a fierce look. They both identified themselves and showed their badges off.

"My name is Chester Foxglove." said the little man. He was slight and balding. "I work in the accounting department at Scotland Yard and I investigate financial fraud crimes. This is not my case- except the villain has been using my name. When your Constable, Mr Cheswick contacted me I was shocked and promised to help him apprehend this man."

"My name is Detective Inspector Wallace Hunt of Scotland Yard." the stout man said "Orton Black is our number one priority- or, rather, he was, until your Constable here apprehended him. Constable

Cheswick contacted us several months ago when your local robbery spree began. He knew right away who Orton Black was and laid out a plan to capture him."

Detective Inspector Hunt turned to Cheswick, "Constable?"

This was such a turn of events, no one noticed the rain or the wind or the occasional thunder now. The town, gathered, listened in rapt attention as Caleb Cheswick- a new Cheswick it seemed to them- began to explain what had happened.

"Orton Black's intention all along was to steal the remaining fortune from the Devil's Elbow. When the little robberies began in the spring- with no evidence and no trace of entry or exit, we were certain he had come, but we had no idea Mr Rampert's role in it all. That was when I contacted Detective Inspector Hunt. It was clear he was looking for clues which might lead him to the fortune he sought. It wasn't difficult to identify him as Orton Black- since he was the only stranger in town I didn't personally invite. We suspected there was no Inspector Foxglove- so I confirmed this with Scotland Yard- he had adopted that personage up to gain public access and to explain his sudden presence.

"Protocol demanded I needed to bring in an expert; I was fully expecting Black to take the bait and he did- he had created the demand himself, of course, by committing the crimes in the first place. I sent a false telegram, liberally letting the public know I would do so. Orton Black intercepted the telegram.

The Wedding Day

He sent a reply pretending to be Scotland Yard, telling me to expect an inspector by the name of Foxglove, and showed up on my doorstep right on schedule.

"But of course, though we were certain Orton Black was the criminal in the Germany and Spain murders and that Foxglove was really Orton Black- we had no proof of any of it. We had to get real evidence so we went along with his plan, letting him think he was in charge and having his way. We gave him as much leniency as we thought was safe to conduct his crime in the name of justice.

"But he turned arsonist and burned to the ground the Pimsleur estate. I think he suspected then the Pimsleur estate was where the treasure was.

"It was Foxglove's idea to frame me for the arson, which didn't surprise me, and send me to London. Of course, the moment I got to London, I turned right around and returned to Westwich by the next train, after fooling Black's cronies in London into thinking I had gone to the ratty hostel he had set up for me, where he could keep an eye on me.

"I arranged for visitors at the hostel in London, to keep up appearances. Meanwhile, I was hiding in the cottage on the Huffington-In-Box estate, keeping an eye on Black's progress as Foxglove. I enlisted the help of the Vagabonds to help me in this, and they did a spectacular work on my behalf. More than once this past week they distracted the Brigade while I moved from one place to another.

"When I heard he had figured out who Mr Rampert really was, I knew I had to move quickly. I spoke secretly to Mr Rampert and told him my plan to let Black know about the treasure and where to find it, and then after Black got his clues from Rampert, we pretended a kidnapping for Foxglove's benefit. I wanted to draw him to the cottage.

"It took him longer than I thought it would to find me at the cottage, but he is a criminal after all; more accustomed to running and hiding than chasing and finding. Just as we planned, he found Mr Rampert by himself in the cottage. I was in hiding until I heard him plainly implicate himself, and then I apprehended him. We wrestled but I put the handcuffs on him."

Niles Blankenship spoke up.

"Mr Cheswick, you keep saying 'we', not 'I'. Who else was with you in this elaborate capture?"

"That was me." Penelope Pimsleur said. She stepped forward. "Caleb needed someone who wouldn't be suspected of involvement. Caleb and I pretended to have a falling out- not even my parents knew what we were really planning- so there would be no one who would think we were working together. Plus, I know all the hiding places in the neighborhood. Caleb and I could meet in any of a dozen places no one else knows. I kept him updated on Foxglove and the movements of the Brigade as well. I owe you an apology, a public one at that, Mr Blankenship. I'm afraid I cannot marry you- I am spoken for already. It was a cruel farce, and I am sorry." Penelope said.

"But Penelope! My unrequited love-!" Niles Blankenship began to say.

But Penelope interrupted him, "Their is no dowry in trust, Mr Blankenship. I made it up." And those standing nearby saw Niles love swiftly requited.

Now Hunt and Foxglove (the real one, from the financial fraud cases) each took Orton Black by an arm and hauled him to his feet roughly.

The face of Orton Black was livid, but childish. It was clear he had never been caught at anything before and it was a new experience for him. Professional mastermind that he was, the sensation of capture was brand new- he was an amateur in custody. He tried to stomp and lash his way out, but ineffectually. They took him out the door and into the rain, where a carriage waited.

"I'll be back!" Orton Black shouted. "You haven't seen the last of me!"

But somehow, they all knew he wouldn't- and they most certainly had.

***

In the days and weeks that followed, Westwich and the surrounding neighbourhood began to return to its old self. There are a few things that happened worth telling about. The aftermath of the storm was cleaned up and no one would worry about firewood for some time.

Mrs B was the first to throw a party and even the Pimsleurs were invited. In fact, Mrs B had asked Laura Pimsleur to join her in the planning of the event- and it was, by all accounts, an excellent party.

Hildegard Pimsleur, in a story rather unrelated to anything we have spoken of here, met a handsome banker who was a family friend. Their marriage was arranged for a time when the family could all be in London next. Her work as a nanny- which she was minimally suited for- came to an end and she became instead a favorite aunt to the children, without the trouble or difficulties of discipline and education.

Mr Bruce Harold and his wife Rebecca found new respect from the Harold family at large, having been so near one of the crime stories of the century and living to tell the tale. They were invited to the next Christmas where it was discovered Bruce and Rebecca had even been victims of the notorious Orton Black- he had actually been in their home and identified items of such value that he took them for himself!

"He was a thiefer of the highest order, I'll give him that. But his elementary grasp of the English language was a poor cover for one supposed to be so clever." Mr Harold told them.

It was Bruce, then, who expanded the facts just enough to drop humble hints he might have had a hand in the actual apprehension of Orton Black.

Never a straightforward statement or admission, just enough to let others know he couldn't really talk about the particulars; not as a gentlemen, who shouldn't talk about himself and if the authorities were mum on it, well, no gentleman needs the publicity of celebrity, do they?

And so Mr Bruce Harold and his wife, Rebecca grew in the estimation of the rest of the Harolds and if they weren't quite so wealthy or influential as the others, no matter, as they contributed to society in their own way.

Mr Rampert, now his secret was known- there was no keeping it now- began a vigorous campaign of philanthropy. He had experienced first hand the danger of closely-held wealth and the fear of the experience never left him. Anytime he felt the spectre of it rise up, another workhouse, orphanage or other charity received a sizable donation. He was cured from then on of his cough for several years- until a real cough caught up with him.

Mr Silverstonne continued to resent the postal tax.

Arthur Denton, champion smoker, became the youngest Constable's Assistant in Westwich (and surrounding neighbourhood) in anyone's memory. His experience with the Vagabonds helped his reputation immensely and when it came time, years later, he was the obvious choice to become the new Constable and though he never solved any international conspiracies or put any notorious criminals behind bars, he kept the honest people of Westwich honest.

Now, we should say a few last words.

First, Orton Black was sent to London where he was convicted of crimes- too many to list here- committed all over England. He was sentenced to spend the rest of his days locked in the Tower. Before the sentence was to begin, of course, he was extradited to eight other countries where he had committed heinous acts. The sentences handed down in those courts were all life sentences as well; to be served consecutively.

Niles Blankenship and his sister, Prunaprismia, now deeply disenchanted with life in Westwich, became missionaries in Darkest Africa where, we are sorry to report, they did very well for themselves.

Father Leamas studiously gathered his notes on the evolution of the human eye and published a paper which did well in literary circles, but never really gained any meaningful traction in serious academic or scientific fields.

And finally, for very nearly single-handedly capturing Orton Black red-handed, Caleb Cheswick was given the Blue Cross by Scotland Yard and granted the honorary title of Master Detective, along with a pleading invitation to move to London and work with them exclusively. He politely declined.

Then, and this took a week or two to really come about, the Master Detective was awarded an honor from the Crown itself, granting him the title of Lord

Cheswick (for invaluable services rendered to the crown and given with deepest gratitude) along with the sizable plot of land beyond the south road- across from the Pimsleur's home- and an income well beyond anything which anyone in Westwich had imagined before.

And, as if his own country's gratitude weren't enough, the governments of those countries in which Orton Black had spread terror, including Germany and Spain, sent him honorariums. Within weeks therefore, Caleb Cheswick was wealthy, well-respected and considered a friend of the court in Buckingham Palace, the Palace in Madrid, and the Chancellor in Germany, with pending invitations to visit several heads of state across the Continent; which he planned to accept.

So it was the following spring that Lord Cheswick and Penelope Pimsleur were married on a piece of land newly cleared out for the building of their new home- just across the South Road from where the Pimsleur Estate was being rebuilt in earnest thanks to a small portion of the reward Cheswick had received. Father Leamas performed the ceremony with great skill and simplicity, with only a few scant references to the light and the way it refracted in the eyes of the two young people.

And that is how the famous Lord Cheswick came into his title and his marriage to Penelope Pimsleur- the very same Lord and Lady Cheswick whose great grandson, Lord Easton Cheswick, was in so many important stories of his own.

It was weeks or maybe even months later after their wedding that Lord and Lady Cheswick were sitting in the garden. Dinner was over and the guests, only a few that evening, had already gone home, and the memory of all that had transpired the previous year seemed to come back over Lady Cheswick as she sat with her husband.

"Caleb, do you know that you are the bravest man in Westwich?" she asked.

Lord Cheswick had smiled a more sheepish smile than she had ever seen. "My dearest Penelope," he said "do you remember the day I met you and your sister on the road last spring- and I had asked if you had seen any suspicious characters following you?"

"I remember it well. I was so grateful you had been there to protect us!" Lady Cheswick said. "I suppose that was Orton Black, even then, plotting his evil scheme all the while!"

Lord Cheswick shook his head.

"It was me, Pen. I had been wanting to see you again and couldn't get up the courage. So I followed you. I was worried you might see me, and I was trying to come up with a reason to talk to you. I made up a story about a suspicious character in which a constable would have to be involved professionally. I'm afraid I'm not very brave, after all." Lord Cheswick said.

And that is the story of the legendary battle of wits between the famous detective, Inspector Foxglove and the infamous criminal, Orton Black which took place in the little town of Westwich; and how the infamous criminal was, in the end, apprehended and brought to justice by the true Master Detective.

Made in United States
Troutdale, OR
05/10/2025